Green
en, Katherine
reak in the family tree

$24.99
on1385364460

DISCARD

A Freak in the Family Tree

by
Katherine Green

This is a work of fiction. Name, characters, places, and incidents are either the product of the author's imagination or are used fictitiously, and any resemblance to actual persons, living or dead, business establishments, events, or locales is entirely coincidental.

Copyright © 2021

All rights reserved. No part of this book may be reproduced, transmitted, or stored in an information retrieval system in any form or by any means electronic, mechanical, photocopying, recording, or otherwise, without written permission from the author.

Library of Congress Cataloging-in-Publication Data available upon request.
Name, Green, Katherine, author.
Title: A Freak in the Family Tree

Identifiers: LCCN 2022909690 (print)
ISBN 978-0-9861825-1-8 (hard cover)

Subjects: Fiction l Adventure l Family Tree l Fantasy l Historical Fiction
Ages 12 and up

For my sister Shirley and her insights
For my mom, a loving first-grade teacher
For Auntie Jo, a dedicated sixth-grade teacher
For Uncle Carl, an intrepid grade school principal
For Uncle James, a worthy college professor
For my sister Peggy, a classical pianist who performs,
teaches, and implements educational programs in the arts.

To teachers everywhere who fight the good fight.
To students everywhere who search for the light.

And to libraries and librarians who serve us all.
Vive les livres!

Chapters

1 Prologue i
2 The Curse 1
3 The Jump 9
4 Bicycle Thief 13
5 Family Secret 19
6 Racist 23
7 Stargazers 27
8 Pony Phonies 33
9 Hunk Help 39
10 The Prank 44
11 The Shot 49
12 Busted! 52
13 The Hidey-hole 58
14 New Stepmom 61
15 The Makeover 67
16 Through the Knothole 72
17 The Higglby Tree 77
18 No Guts, No Glory 82
19 The Mad Scientist 87
20 Tree Begone 93
21 The Cherrywood Box 96
22 Tree for Two 100
23 The Bundle 106
24 A Man, a Plan... 112
25 Keys, Please 118

26	Brave Old World	125
27	Wagon Ho!	131
28	The Awakening	138
29	Baubles, Bangles, and	145
30	Burglary	145
31	The River	149
32	Another Higglby	156
33	Visitors	163
34	Stolen!	172
35	Questions	175
36	The Six Grandfathers	180
37	Gone!	186
38	Gold Fever	189
39	The Chase	195
40	Beyond the Beyond	201
41	Stablemates	208
42	Homecoming	213
43	Killing Snakes	222
44	The Braidy Bunch	228
45	Grace Under Pressure	232
46	The Jump-off	237
47	The Knockdown	243
48	The Takedown	248
49	Shock and Awe	252

Prologue

I glanced behind me. The bike thief was still there.

My lungs were about to burst as I neared my house. Only a block to go—but that block was straight uphill. I heard him coming up behind me…

※

Peerless the Plunderer leaned down like a teacher getting ready to shake his finger in my face—a gesture I'm familiar with. "You a Higglby?" he asked gruffly.

"Yes."

"You can see this tree?"

"Yes."

"Then you're dead."

I'd heard enough. All I wanted was to get out of there. I turned and dove headfirst out of the knothole and landed back in the Forbidden Forest. I didn't care where I was going as long as it was away from that tree!

1
The Curse

Having homework on the last week of school is outrageous. But this assignment was the worst ever! Research my family tree. People in this town already know too much about the Higglby family tree. It should be fed into a wood chipper, not put on display in a sixth-grade classroom.

I heard Mrs. Dixon say, "Is something wrong, Kit?"

I snapped out of my funk. The other kids had left the room, and I was sitting there like the last cracker on a cheese plate. I wanted to yell, "This assignment is bull pucky!" But all I said was, "No, ma'am." Cowardice is part of the Higglby curse.

I left the room and headed for my safe space—my locker. Here, I am queen. And my locker is my castle! I designed it myself.

The top two-thirds is a vanity table: nail polish, designer water bottle, and makeup to cover the three big Higglby freckles on the bridge of my nose. Old photos show all Higglbys had them, and all old Higglbys were losers.

A guitar is also taking up locker space. I chose orchestra as an elective, and chose the guitar because it looks the way *I* want to look—a curvy body with a long, slender neck. Unfortunately, playing guitar requires practice, so, no, I can't play—but when I shake it, there are three picks rattling around inside that sound a lot like maracas.

The bottom third of my locker is books and binders. The books were an afterthought because I'm not exactly honor roll material. But my binder covers are outstanding!

The motto I wrote this week on the dry-erase board inside my locker door says:

You miss 100% of the shots you never take.

—Wayne Gretzky

I checked my hair in the lighted makeup mirror above the board. It looked the same as it did this morning and every morning, sitting on my head like a big ball of cheap red yarn. Dad calls it "the Higglby hair"—all part of the Higglby curse.

That said, you might as well know my first name. It's Kitten. Dad named me that because he thought I was cute as one. But after barely surviving kindergarten with that name, I shortened it to Kit.

Above the mirror are pics of my three best friends since preschool. Now we're finishing our first year in middle school, and we're still BFFs. At least, I think we are.

Lately when I glance at that photo, I get a thud in the pit of my stomach. I can't shake the feeling they've been snubbing me. It may be because they're planning European vacations this summer. Me? As usual, I'll be staying across town at the Higglby farm. I won't even be leaving Connecticut.

I started for the lunchroom still upset about that family tree assignment and still mad at being stuck with the name Higglby.

My mom's new name is Prescott. You can't go wrong with that name in this town. Stuart Prescott, my stepdad, makes a lot of money as a corporate lawyer, which is why I get to go to a private school like Wilderidge Hall.

My real dad? He's a junk man. Max Higglby buys junk—old, useless junk. How Mom ended up with him is a story for another day. But the divorce judge said I have to keep his last name until I turn thirteen. The good news is I turn thirteen this summer. The bad news is the family tree assignment is due in two days.

So I was up to my neck in disgust when the school jerkwad passed me. Every school has one—a kid who's more annoying than a rabid hyena but not as cute. In my school, that kid is Jonathan Rimroth Jr., a guy so full of himself he probably has to weigh himself twice.

Today his goon is with him, a kid everyone calls Bulldozer. Dozer always sits behind me in assembly chewing bubble gum in my ear. Rumor is his father's in the mob. I doubt that's true, but in case it is, I've never told him to quit popping his gum. Why should I be the one to wake up in a trunk full of burner phones and a bag full of snakes?

I heard Jonathan's obnoxious voice exploding out of his cork-shaped head. "Well, if it isn't Kit Kat, the junkyard rat. Move it, loser."

He gave me a shove, followed by a laugh that always sounded like someone machine-gunning a bag of wet socks.

In kindergarten, when I heard that rhyme, it made me cry. Now it just makes me mad—and I was already mad.

"Has your dad stolen any more city funds lately?" I snapped.

Bad idea. Jonathan turned on me like a hopped up howler monkey.

"That charge was never proven, just alleged!"

"Your head is a ledge!" I shot back. Another bad idea.

I watched his fleshy face turn from salmon pink to candy apple red. Coward that I am, I quickly ducked into the lunchroom where a teacher was pulling guard duty. Rimroth decided not to push his luck.

As I got in line, I saw Valerie heading to where the other Rein Bows were sitting. That's the name of our horse-riding club. One reason we've always been such good friends is our love of horses. We're all members of the Silver Saddles Riding Academy.

To keep the record straight, I don't own a horse; my mom does. But she lets me ride her, and groom her, and love her.

Valerie is the leader of our group. There's something about Val that makes you notice her whether you want to or not, like a speed bump—only it's your eyes that slow down.

Valerie is fearless. She wouldn't have ducked Jonathan. She would've hung him by the seat of his pants on the Wildcat statue in the foyer.

I piled some sweet-and-sour chicken on my tray and headed for our table. Other kids were there too, so I wedged in between Crystal and Blaine.

There was that feeling again. No mention that I'd joined them. They just kept talking about the horse-jumping contest at Silver Saddles in a couple of weeks.

I wondered if that was why they'd been giving me the cold shoulder. They think I'm acting like a baby because I don't like horse jumping. But I have a good reason for not wanting to jump over a fence on a horse—fear of dying! I've seen riders crash and burn on those fences. No, thank you!

I was hoping they'd be talking about something else—like maybe the cute guy we saw at Crandall's Creamery the other day. I tried changing the subject from horse jumping to Creamery Hunk.

"Let's go by Crandall's after school and see if that total hunk shows up again," I chimed in.

"He isn't a regular or we would've seen him before," Crystal said dismissively.

"I concur," Valerie added with her usual swag. "But he was *trés magnifique.*"

That means "very magnificent" in French. Val has started throwing French phrases around. I find it trés annoying, but she doesn't care what people think of her. It's only important what she thinks of them.

Crystal took a bite of her sandwich like it might bite her back. "God, I wish they'd serve real food here!" She tried to sound angry, but everything she says comes out like soft-serve ice cream. It's no secret that Crystal is the boy magnet of the group. Blaine just sat there scrolling on her cell phone.

If my friends seem a little shallow, that's because they are. We all are. I'm not bragging, just explaining—a task that usually falls to me since I'm the smartest of the four of us—and I'm barely dragging a C+ average this year.

Since they didn't want to talk about cute guys, I brought up an uncute one. "I just had a run-in with Jonathan Rimroth. I am so sick of him and that stupid chant."

"Well, what do you expect?" Crystal said. "I mean you *are* a Higglby."

A thud in my stomach began to ooze through my whole body. The four of us had become friends because of our love for horses. But for me, another important bond that held us together was that they'd never made fun of me for being a Higglby. Had that bond just been broken?

"We're veering off topic," Valerie said sharply. "We need to get some jumping in. I've seen that stupid Filly Phosphorescent club practicing at Silver Saddles. I'd die if they beat us."

"Those lightweights?" Blaine chirped. "I could outride them on a hobbyhorse."

"No harm in making sure," Valerie insisted. "Let's meet tomorrow after school. We've only got a few weeks before the competition."

"I'm ready!" Crystal smiled. Then her eyes swiveled to me. "But I think Kit is still afraid." She brushed back a strand of her honey-colored hair to make sure they didn't miss her smirk.

"I'm not afraid; my horse is," I lied.

The moment I said it, I felt guilty for blaming Grace. Grace is my mom's beautiful chestnut horse, and she loves to jump. I'm the one who starts shaking like a tuning fork at the thought. But I wasn't about to tell them that.

"I'll be there tomorrow," I said like I meant it. "Maybe I can get her over a small jump." I tried to swallow a chunk of chicken along with that commitment, but it fought me all the way down.

Val suddenly gasped. "Omigod! Gwen said I could copy her English homework. Do I still have time?" She was wearing a Cartier bracelet watch, but she fished her phone out of her backpack to check the time. Either way, lunch was over.

I spent all fifth hour wondering how in the flaming fudge I could get over my fear of jumping by tomorrow afternoon. The only way would be to practice today after school.

I'd watched Valerie sail her horse, Sheba, over a jump and come gracefully down on the other side. I'd pretend it was me gliding through the air. But it never was.

I was jolted from my daydream by an announcement over the PA system—a warning to be alert for bicycle thieves. Someone had been knocking kids off their bikes, then stealing the bike. We were urged not to ride alone.

Son of a monkey! If I biked to the riding academy after school to secretly practice jumping, I'd have to go alone. Maybe if I rode fast, no bike thief could catch me.

The bell was still clanging when I grabbed my bike and headed for Silver Saddles faster than a cheetah full of chili peppers. I thought about taking the backstreets to make sure none of the Rein Bows saw where I was going. But backstreets are probably where bike thieves hang out so I stuck to the main road.

Usually, I loved going to the riding academy. Just knowing Grace would be there to greet me put a smile on my face.

There's something unique about a horse. They don't give you unconditional love like dogs do. You have to earn a horse's love. But if one ever puts its big, beautiful head on your shoulder, or blows a gentle puff of air in your face—their version of a kiss—then you know a horse is a special animal.

But on this trip I wasn't thinking about the horse. After a few blocks, I even forgot about the bicycle thieves. The only thought pulsating in my brain was the jump.

My stomach was on churn but I'd made up my mind. Falling might hurt, but losing my friends would hurt a lot more.

2
The Jump

When I arrived at Silver Saddles, I smiled at the lush, manicured grounds. This was my fantasy world! All the sights and smells stirred up wonderful memories. I know how lucky I am. And I know how different my life would be if I'd grown up on Dad's run-down old farm on the other side of town.

I love Dad. I love how he's comfortable in his own skin, and how he doesn't just live life, he acts like he invented it. But the life I'm living now suits me more.

I was four when Mom remarried and moved us across town where the rich kids live. Now I have my own room with a big-screen TV. I'm not like Blaine, who binge-watches *The Vampire Diaries* on her cell phone; I like my screen big! I also like having designer clothes, a fancy school, and occasional parties—none of which I'd have if Mom hadn't moved to greener pastures, literally.

I checked the jumping arena. The Filly Phosphorescents, our archrivals from a nearby town, were there. Val says their parents have money, but not Wilderidge money. They sometimes jumped at Silver Saddles, but I didn't know any of them, so no need to impress. I'd just throw on a T-shirt and go for it.

On my way to the locker room, I saw a stable boy scooping poop and asked him to saddle the horse in stall four.

"Sure thing," he said, glancing up at me.

OMG! It was the guy from Crandall's Creamery—and even cuter than I remembered. His shirtsleeves were cut off at the shoulder—or maybe ripped off by his biceps. He was wearing a cowboy hat, and when he looked up from under the brim, his eyes were like chocolate parfait.

Change of plans! Creamery Hunk's presence called for a much better wardrobe. I hurried to the locker room and changed into riding pants, bright white and formfitting. I don't have much form to fit, but I look more grown up in them.

I was reaching for my dress white riding shirt when a thought pierced my brain. This guy works at a stable. The richer I look, the worse he might feel.

I've started thinking about stuff like that lately. Like, what kind of person do I want to be? And do I like who I am now?

Last month I asked Eliana, our housekeeper, what "white privilege" was and she said, "You." So-o-o was that a pat on my back or a sarcastic slam? Unanswered questions.

I went with a casual riding shirt. But as I dressed, my eyes fell on an inflatable safety vest I'd never worn lying in the bottom of the locker. That's when reality smacked me in the face. I was getting ready to go flying over a fence on a horse without falling off!

I began to wish I had Valerie's confidence...or was it aloofness? Whatever it was, I wish I had it, but I don't. I put on the safety vest. It actually looked pretty good on me. Besides, Creamery Hunk wouldn't be interested in a corpse, so win-win! I pulled on my riding boots, grabbed my helmet, and headed for Grace's stall.

Grace was saddled and waiting outside. No Creamery Hunk was in sight, but he'd tied Grace's reins with an excellent quick-release knot—I'm sort of an expert on knots. But right now, I had bigger whales to fry.

My nerves ran laps around my spine as I took Grace through her warm up paces in the arena. I zeroed in on a three-foot jump painted like a candy cane and remembered my coach saying, "*Stick your booty in the air like you don't even care!*" I also remembered my dry-erase board motto: *You miss 100% of the shots you never take.*

I turned Grace toward the jump while wishing I had muscles in my legs instead of two toothpicks dangling in the stirrups. But there was no way to grow any now. It was Go Time!

I prodded Grace into a canter. As the jump got closer, I counted the rhythm: four...three...two...panic! I did the worst thing possible—I pulled back on the reins. Grace followed the command and stopped short, but I didn't. I went flying over Grace's head and landed flat on my back on the other side of the jump.

People began to stare, so I scrambled to my feet and yelled, "Ta-da!" to show them I was fine. And I was—until I looked down and saw I had peed my pants!

I hopped back on Grace and left the arena hoping no one had noticed—especially Creamery Hunk.

I ran into the locker room. Minutes ago, I thought tight white pants made me look grown-up—not so much when you pee them. I glared in the mirror. A big yellow spot glared back at me.

I stripped off the riding pants and underwear and buried them deep in the trash. Then I pulled on my jeans, grabbed my backpack, and went to put Grace in her stall.

She was still tied in front of the locker area, but she wasn't alone. Standing there patting her neck was Creamery Hunk. I managed a weak smile.

"Could you put her up for me? I'm late for dinner."

"Can do," he said. But as I turned to leave, he added, "Are you sure you're okay?"

Son of a monkey! He'd seen the whole thing. "I'm fit as a fiddle, just running late. See ya!"

Fit as a fiddle? Did that come out of my mouth? I grabbed my bike and headed home.

3
Bicycle Thief

So it was over between Creamery Hunk and me before I even knew his name. What's worse, I'd chickened out of the jump again.

Suddenly, I realized I had a bigger problem. I was chugging past Trumble Middle School when some Black dude raced across the parking lot toward me. Trumble is the public middle school so I didn't know anyone from there.

I decided to ignore him, but when I glanced over my shoulder, a boulder-sized lump formed in my throat. He'd left the parking lot and was coming up fast behind me wearing a tinted visor over his face. The words *bicycle thief* and *don't ride alone* began running on a loop in my brain.

I picked up speed as I reached Wendom Hills Estates, where I live. Most homes are gated, so I couldn't just race up to someone's door and yell for help. My best bet was to put pedal to the metal and get to my house before he got to me!

I made a sharp turn onto my street, but two things were working against me. One: my whole body was beginning to ache from the failed jump. Two: They weren't kidding when they named this place Wendom Hills. I was pumping like mad, but the hill was winning.

I glanced behind me. The bike thief was still there. Now I knew he was after me because I'd never seen a Black family in Wendom Hills—and very few in Wilderidge. Another time, I might have wondered why, but this didn't feel like the right moment to sort that out.

My lungs were about to burst as I neared my house. Only a block to go—but that block was straight uphill. I heard him coming up behind me, but before I could decide what to do, the thief blew past me and swung into my driveway. By the time I got there, someone had opened the door and let him in! This was too weird for words.

As I dragged my aching body toward the house, I noticed my stepdad's car in the driveway. He was never home this early—but there he was in the living room. And so was a woman in a lab coat and hospital scrubs.

Barrister turned when I wobbled in the front door. Barrister is what I call my stepdad. That's what they call lawyers in England, so he's cool with it.

"Kathleen, your mom had an accident, but she'll be fine. She's in her room, resting. Mrs. Sheppard will be staying with her till the night nurse gets here."

Kathleen is what Barrister calls *me*. He doesn't care for Kitten or Kit, so he goes with my middle name, Kathleen.

Then he told me about Mom's latest adventure. She'd gone hang gliding and crashed into a mobile home. Mom is always doing screwball stuff. Her body is like a slow cooker, but her brain is set on microwave.

"Can I see her?" I asked, looking up at Barrister's perfect gray hair above his charcoal-gray suit and Windsor-knotted tie. The man could be a mannequin.

"Not right now," he said, meeting my gaze. He always met your gaze. "She just got home from the hospital, and the medication hasn't worn off yet."

Barrister glanced out the window. "That isn't where your bike belongs, young lady." His cell phone buzzed as he left the room.

My mom is the exact opposite of my stepdad. He's got a button-down personality. She's a total flake. Oddly enough, she's also the exact opposite of my real dad. He owns one suit and keeps duct tape in the breast pocket. Maybe she just likes living in other people's worlds.

Mrs. Sheppard, the nurse, was still standing there. She was a Black lady with shortish dark hair wearing a pair of rimless glasses. She looked at me and smiled. You know how when some people smile, you feel like they're almost hugging you with it? This woman had that kind of smile. I would have followed her anywhere.

"Your mama's going to be just fine, and I'll be here every day to make sure of that."

"Your name is Shepherd and you're a nurse," I pointed out. "That's cool."

She looked perplexed.

"You take care of people like shepherds take care of sheep," I explained.

Mrs. Sheppard's eyes twinkled. "You know, I never thought about that—maybe because I spell it a little differently. But that is a very astute observation. What does Prescott mean?"

I got a knot in my stomach—probably a monkey's knot, very hard to untie. "That's my stepdad's name. Mine is Higglby...I don't think it has a meaning."

An odd look flickered over Mrs. Sheppard's face. "Kit Higglby?" she asked.

I nodded, wondering how she knew, but I didn't care once that smile of hers returned.

"Maybe your name is one of a kind," she said. "That makes you even more special. And just look at those emerald eyes of yours. I hope you always keep a smile in them because they sure do shine."

I was beginning to love this woman.

"I hope we have time to talk later, but you better get your bike moved," she suggested.

True. Barrister didn't like having to tell you things twice. I left, still thinking about my emerald eyes. That was one Higglby trait I actually liked. Dad calls them "screamin' green," but I think I like "emerald" better.

I was moving my bike when I saw the bike thief who apparently wasn't one. Not only that, she was a girl! With her helmet off, I couldn't believe I'd mistaken her for a boy. She looked about my age and had silky black hair to die for—if I were the envious type.

She probably straightens it, I thought, but in almost the same thought bubble I remembered thinking about having mine straightened. I promptly filed that thought in a drawer in my brain—a drawer I didn't know I needed—labeled "Hypocritical Snob."

"Hi, I'm Kit." I offered as a conversation starter.

"I'm Whitney," she said as she put her bike on the rack of a car parked in the turnaround.

"You must be with Mom's nurse?"

"I'm waiting for her to get off work."

This girl was clearly not running for Miss Congeniality, so I went to my room and took a hot shower. But even that didn't wash away the humiliation I felt as I remembered my fall in front of Creamery Hunk. Born to lose, I reminded myself. All part of the Higglby curse!

I came downstairs and saw Whitney's things in the den. She'd left a book open on the table. The Title read *Les Trois Mousquetaires*. I was pretty sure it was *The Three Musketeers*, but OMG! She was reading it in the original French! I barely got through the movie in the original English!

Mom and I often had dinner alone, but this time it was Barrister and me. Our small talk was dull, even for small talk. I thought about Whitney. She wasn't exactly a chatterbox, but she must be bored with homework by now.

"The nurse's daughter is here; should we invite her to eat with us?"

I'm not allowed to have my phone at the table, but Barrister was constantly checking his tonight. He didn't look up. "Eliana said she's already eaten. I'm sure she's fine."

She might be fine, but I wasn't. Guilt was gnawing at me for assuming she was a bike thief. After dinner, I went back to the den. Whitney was there studying.

"Hi again," I said. She gave me a "Hi" back, but when I didn't leave, she looked up.

"Don't *you* have homework to do?"

"Just some family tree junk, but it isn't due until Wednesday. I kind of wanted to apologize. When I saw you behind me on my way home, I thought you were trying to steal my bike."

She looked at me like I was shallow as a pie plate. "I have one," she said coolly.

"Well, obviously," I shot back. "But, you know—it's not as nice."

"It's nicer than you are." Her tone got colder. "It's never accused me of being a thief."

I was about to storm off when Mrs. Sheppard walked in. "Kit, your mama's awake. She'd like to see you."

"Thank you." I shot Whitney my best go-to-the-devil look and left in a huff disguised as disinterest.

4
Family Secret

Mom had already drifted back to sleep when I entered. It was odd seeing her lying there in a hospital gown instead of a satin chemise. Her hair and makeup looked like they'd been through a wind tunnel, but at least she was home from the hospital.

Her bedroom reminded me of a princess's room in a fairy tale. The coolest thing was an oil painting of a woman with big eyes wearing a gold dress that blended into a yellow-gold chair which blended into a solid gold background. The painting was a real eye-catcher.

To kill time, I tried on Mom's jewelry. As I modeled a Tiffany lavaliere necklace in the mirror, I heard Mom's groggy voice.

"See anything you like?"

"I'd like to know what you were thinking…hang gliding, Mom?"

She tried to move and let out a groan. "I should have stuck to horseback jumping," she whispered, then added dreamily:

> "By firefly light in a star-filled trance,
> The clouds will swirl, and the woods will dance.
> And I will dream of wonderful things
> Like taking flight on gossamer wings."

She looked at me sheepishly. "I crashed into a mobile home. You should've seen the family come running out."

"What did you say to them?"

"I said, 'I'm home!'"

We laughed, then Mom sighed. "I've been doing a lot of things I have no business doing at my age—maybe because I was too busy to do them when I was younger."

"Busy doing what?"

"Raising you, for one. I hope I didn't mess you up too much."

I shrugged. "So far, so good."

Her eyes closed, but her mouth kept moving. "While my friends were dating in college, I was changing diapers and watching the Muppets…Fozzie Bear was my favorite."

"Mine too."

We laughed again, then Mom opened her eyes and stared at the ceiling.

"You're the best thing that ever happened to me. But now that you're older and spending more time with your friends, I think I'm trying to make up for missing my 'growing up' years. And that's why your mom flew into the side of a house."

She closed her eyes again. "I did some really dumb things in high school. It's insane to think you're in love with someone when you're that young."

Mom laid her head on the pillow and looked up at her memories. "I was prom queen, and he was the star quarterback. He was so handsome…" Her voice trailed off. "I did do one great thing…I had you. I'm sorry your dad and I couldn't make things work. But that's water under the bridge. Now I've got Stuart—or Barrister, as you call him. And your dad has that new—what's her name?"

"Angie, I think." I acted unsure, but I knew her name. I'd met her last summer when I was at Dad's. She was nice but a junkaholic just like Dad. That's how they met: She opened an antique shop in town. Dad brought in stuff to resell. Bang! New stepmom.

"I'm glad we're living here instead of at the farm. I'm not a farm kind of girl."

"Me neither." She closed her eyes again. "I've never told you this, but the farm wasn't the only reason I left your father. One day, something happened to him." She turned her head away.

This was no time for clamming up. "What happened?" I prodded.

"Our house had a little fireplace. He liked to chop the wood for it."

I gasped, "Did he go to the Forbidden Forest?"

"Oh, quit calling it that," she scolded. "People think the Higglbys are crazy enough without spreading those tales."

She was right, but it's been called that ever since my great-grandfather inherited the Higglby farm.

"So, what happened?" I asked again.

Mom took a deep breath that didn't stop until she'd sucked every ounce of air from her lungs.

"All I know is when he came back, he didn't have any firewood, and he was…different. He just stood there pale as a ghost. I swear I could see right through his eyes to the back of his head. But all he said was 'I saw a tree.'"

"He saw a tree?" I repeated. "He went to the woods and saw a tree, and it scared him?"

She nodded. "Then your great-granddad died, and Max tells me we're moving to the farm without even discussing it! That's when I decided it was time for you and me to start a new life somewhere else." She squeezed my hand. "But your dad loves you. He misses you a lot."

"I know. But I still don't like being called a junkyard rat."

Mom gave a half laugh. "Don't tell your stepdad they call you that. He might sue them."

"Fine with me!" I sniffed.

Mom smiled a goofy smile. I think the meds were wearing off. "Your first dad's advice is better. He always says a person has to kill his own snakes."

"Meaning?"

"Meaning fight your own battles…I think your dad is still trying to fight one of his. He just won't tell anyone what it is."

Mrs. Sheppard walked in. "Sorry to interrupt, but your mama needs her rest. She's had a rough day."

I couldn't argue with that.

5
Racist

My day hadn't been all unicorns and candy either. I'd mucked up the jump—not to mention my underwear—made a mortal enemy of Jonathan Rimroth, then found out my dad might be coming unhinged like *his* dad did.

I felt like I was playing a game of Tetris where none of the pieces fit. I decided to go someplace where I could think.

I wandered into the backyard wondering if my mom had missed so much of her youth she needed gossamer wings to get it back. Was it possible to want to grow up so fast that you end up never growing up at all?

Our hilltop view of the night sky is awesome, so I planted myself in the hanging daybed. I liked to swing back and forth while I stared at the stars. But I was still trying to find the Big Dipper when I realized I wasn't alone. That girl, Whitney, was lying on her back in the grass.

"What are *you* doing out here?" I asked flatly.

"Looking at the stars."

"Me too," I decided to answer.

She pointed to the Big Dipper. "The two stars on the outer bowl of the Big Dipper lead to the North Star, which is the first star on the handle of the Little Dipper."

"I like to look, not learn," I said defensively.

After the silence became deafening, I blurted out, "You think I'm a racist, don't you? Just because I thought you were a bike thief."

"Depends," she said, still watching the sky. "Did you think I was a thief because I was following you? Or because I was Black?"

Whoa! I had to think about that.

"Both?" I admitted. She didn't reply, so I changed the subject. "You're a good cyclist."

"That's because I don't have butlers to chauffeur me around," she snarked.

"*Now* who's being racist?" I snarked back.

"That wasn't racism. It was classism—you're rich, and I'm not."

"We're not rich—well, not rich rich."

Whitney glanced over. "Our class field trip was to the zoo. Where did you go?"

"To the New York Stock Exchange on Wall Street." I couldn't see her eyes, but I'm pretty sure they were laughing at me. "We don't have a chauffeur," I muttered.

"Then maybe I'm a better rider because I don't have those spindly little legs of yours."

"Okay, that was racist!" I said with conviction.

"No, that was conceit. It would be racist if I'd said 'those spindly little *white* legs of yours.' Now, if I added, 'All your muscles are in your rich white head,' that would be racist, classist, *and* conceit—except I saw your science project in the den, so let's classify it as a factual observation."

"Are you calling me stupid?"

"Well, if the IQ fits…" She let that hang.

"Hey, I came out here to look at the stars, so why don't you either leave or shut your black hole—oh, god! I did not mean that like it sounded—it's just the only astronomy term I know."

To my relief, Whitney laughed. "I knew what you meant."

I quickly changed the subject. "Are you new in town?" I was surprised I hadn't seen her around.

"I'm new everywhere. This is my third school in four years. I was a Navy brat." She paused. "My mom and I used to stargaze before she died."

"Oh, I thought Mrs. Sheppard was your mom."

"She's my grandmama. My mom died in some stupid naval training drill."

My eyes widened. "Oh, *she* was the one in the Navy? Bizarre!"

"Oh, racist *and* sexist."

This time, we both laughed.

"Sorry if I'm being rude," I said.

"Same here—and I don't think you're trying to be racist. You're just…"

"Thoughtless?" I proposed.

Whitney nodded. "But with some people it's hard to know. Like, I'm the only Black girl in Honors Science at my school, and some of the guys don't like me. But I don't know if it's because I'm Black or because I'm a girl."

"Could be both. I can't decide if some kids are born mean or get it from their parents."

"Like you said—could be both." Then she added, "Have you read *Lord of the Flies*?"

"Sure," I said, assuming that was the right answer, then added, "Well, I skimmed it," in case there was a follow-up question.

Whitney looked off in the distance. "It reminds me of that line: 'Ralph wept for the end of innocence, the darkness of man's heart, and the fall through the air of the true, wise friend called Piggy.'"

"Who's Piggy?"

She chuckled. "You need to work on your skimming."

Then Mrs. Sheppard called Whitney. She jumped to her feet. "Gotta go." She ran to the front yard, and I heard their car drive away.

This had been some day. I missed a jump, wet my pants, and Mom bashed into a mobile home. Then she tells me Dad got scared because he saw a tree. Yep, definitely one bad freakin' day. What I didn't know was that tomorrow, things would get worse.

6
Stargazers

The next morning before first bell, I saw the Rein Bows huddled at Val's locker sharing pics of some villa in the South of France. Crystal and Blaine's parents had rented it for the summer.

Val just tossed her head. "My plans are up in the air since my parents' separation. But the show jumping finals are in England this year at Windsor Castle, and I wouldn't miss that for the world!"

"Windsor Castle! Ooh! Wouldn't it be fun if we all qualified and got to hang out a few weeks in England this summer?" Crystal squealed. Then she looked at me. "Don't worry, I'm sure you'll have fun at the Higglby farm."

"I can't jump with you guys tonight because my mom was in an accident."

I was hoping their response would show a little pity. But Valerie answered with "No prob. We weren't expecting you."

It wasn't the words; it was the tone. Val had always wielded her tongue like a dagger at kids she didn't like. This time she was stabbing me.

When we were little, the four of us learned to ride bikes together. We played with our Barbies together. And we discovered horses together.

Horses always seemed to like me—I'm not sure my Barbie ever did. The doll always had that look on her face, like deep down in her plastic soul, she knew she was better than me.

But the first time I looked in a horse's eye was the first time I ever shared my ego. And having friends that felt the same way was heaven on earth. God had blown a perfect bubble, and in it were four friends who loved horses. Was that bubble about to burst?

Not if I could help it! If my best friends thought they were outgrowing me, that was a problem I could fix. I spent all first period making a three-part plan.

OPERATION NAME CHANGE: I'll take my stepdad's name as soon as I'm allowed to at the end of the summer. Nobody will mess with Kathleen Prescott!

OPERATION NEW VACATION: I will no longer spend summer break on the Higglby farm after this year. I'll spend it like everyone I know does—posing for selfies in Europe or throwing spectacular pool parties.

OPERATION MAKEOVER: This summer I'll change everything I don't like about my appearance—from the tip of my frizzy hair to the bottom of my spindly legs. *That* will make the Rein Bows realize they've been dissing the wrong girl!

I was still jazzed about my new plan when I got home from school. I was also glad to see Whitney's bike in the drive, but first, I went to visit Mom.

Mrs. Sheppard said she was sleeping but added, "I have a present for you from a little shop in town called Antiques and Abandoned Treasure. Isn't that a cute name?"

I nodded but didn't mention it was my new stepmom's store. I opened the sack. Inside was a strange-looking book.

"I thought it was a sketchbook," Mrs. Sheppard said. "I bought it for Whitney—she's quite an artist. Have you seen the mural she painted on the wall of her school?"

I hadn't.

"Well, it's amazing! But I think this book is too small for her sketches, so maybe you'd like to use it."

"I can't draw."

"Can you write?"

"Of course!" I said, wondering if everyone thought I was dumb as a stump.

"Then maybe you'd enjoy writing in it. It wouldn't be like posting things online. These would be thoughts that belong only to you." She let her dark brown eyes rest on me a moment like she knew something I didn't. "It would be a friend you could always talk to. And no matter what you tell it, it will always agree with you."

I laughed and thanked her, then I blurted out, "I think I said some dumb things to Whitney when we first met. But I wasn't trying to be mean."

"She picks her friends carefully, and she told me she thinks you're okay…for a white girl." Mrs. Sheppard chuckled silently.

"Well, I've had worse reviews," I said. "Is it okay if she has dinner with me? I think we're having lasagna."

"I bet she'd like that. She doesn't hang around with too many people. And everyone can use a friend."

I went to my room and sank down on my bed between two throw pillows to inspect the journal. I liked the way it smelled. The cover was leather with a tooled design of a tree across the front. A strap was woven through the tree to fasten the journal shut. But what was really cool was that all the pages were trimmed in gold. The only other book I'd ever seen like that was a Bible.

If I ever decided to write something special, this is absolutely the book I'd use. I put it in my bookshelf between some unread books, which was pretty much every book there—except for an entire shelf of books about horses. I've read all of them!

Whitney and I had dinner by ourselves in the dining room. But what Eliana put in front of us wasn't lasagna.

"Pot roast? I told everyone we were having lasagna." I pouted.

"Well, you should have told me," Eliana replied.

Whitney took a bite. "If this is pot roast, it's delicious. And if it's lasagna"... She took another bite. "It's still delicious!"

"*Gracias*," Eliana said, then looked at me. "If you want lasagna, I will make some tomorrow, with a side order of *privilegio blanco*." She retreated to the kitchen.

"What did that mean?" I asked.

"Well, blanco means white, so guess what privilegio means?" She giggled.

"A side order of white privilege?" I spluttered. "What does she know about it? She's Mexican or something. Besides, she works for us."

"If you worked for her, would you stop being a human being?"

"No. But while she's here, she's a cook and a housekeeper."

"And a human, and an adult," Whitney added. "When a thankless kid orders her around, her inner mom is bound to come out once in a while."

I stared at Whitney. She stared back.

"You know what I think?" I asked.

"That you'd never hire me as your cook?"

We both started laughing.

After dinner, I apologized to Eliana. Then Whitney and I went outside to do more star watching. We dragged a double chaise lounge onto the lawn and sat back to soak in the night.

"It's cool we both like stargazing," I said.

"Yeah, except I prefer knowing what I'm looking at."

"Not me! I just lie here and let them wash over me. On a really clear night there are so many around me I almost feel like I'm one of them."

Whitney looked at me. "That was poetic. You should write that down."

"Really? Your grandmother says I should write stuff down too…if she really *is* your grandma. She looks too young."

Whitney shrugged. "Like they say, 'Black don't crack.'"

"Well, white sure does. Mom cracked her ribs, her shoulder, and I think part of her butt."

Whitney giggled. "Even you were limping around yesterday."

"I fell off my horse."

She looked at me. "You have a horse?"

"My mom does. Her name is Grace."

Whitney burst out laughing. I didn't see what was funny and said so.

"You fell from Grace," she said. I stared at her.

"It's a biblical reference."

I made a mental note to read more. And that reminded me of something else.

"Do you know what gossamer wings are?" I asked.

"They're like butterfly wings," she answered. "You could've googled that, you know."

"Why google when I know a walking encyclopedia?"

I decided to talk about stuff I couldn't google. I found out Whitney lived with her dad and her grandmother. And that her dad worked at a bakery in town.

Then I told Whitney about the Rein Bows and what good friends we were. And about the Silver Saddles Academy and how fun it was to ride horses.

"If you want, we can go this weekend. You can ride Grace."

Whitney drew back in horror. "Hard pass! To me, a horse is one scary creature."

"How can anyone be scared of something as beautiful as a horse?"

"How can anyone be scared of learning things about the night sky?" she shot back. "And didn't you say you had homework to do…a family tree or something?"

"Yeah, but it's not due until—omigod! Tomorrow!

7
Pony Phonies

I ran to my room, grabbed a piece of paper, and drew a crappy-looking tree. I agonized as I wrote "Higglby Family Tree" at the top. Memories began to flood my brain like a bad storm. All to the soundtrack of a singsong taunt:

Kit Kat, the junkyard rat,
Prowls through garbage like an alley cat.

It isn't just the name people make fun of. The whole family is a joke. I was too young to remember my great-granddad, but word on the street is he was crazier than a two-legged stool in a three-legged race.

Rumor One: One summer, he collected bat poop, which is flammable. He used it to blow up his pickup truck. This claim has been substantiated by a newspaper article Dad saved.

Rumor Two: He made moonshine at the farm. This was never proven.

Rumor Three: He helped a two-headed freak escape from a circus, and it still roams the Forbidden Forest.

Okay, the two-headed freak part is hearsay—but the Forbidden Forest is true. It's a section of woods between the farm and the town that belongs to the Higglby family. It got its name, they say, because Great-granddad planted a land mine or six somewhere on the property so if someone trespassed, they wouldn't do it twice. This also has never been proven—which is a good thing.

I was thinking of just taking an F on this stupid paper when Whitney knocked on the door.

"How's it coming?"

"Not good. How do you draw a nut tree?"

Whitney rolled her eyes. I don't think she has much patience with whiners. And frankly, neither do I.

"Wanna help?" I asked.

She stepped into my room. Then I heard a "Wow!" She took the room in—my desk, computer, walk-in closet, and big-screen TV between huge bookcases filled with dozens of unread books.

I folded my arms. "Don't judge me."

Whitney laughed. "Have you seen this room? How can I not?"

I looked around. "I admit I have an appreciation for some of the nicer things in life. But I don't look down on other people… at least I try not to."

"How did you get to be such an upstanding diva?"

"Maybe because my real dad isn't rich like my stepdad. Or maybe because it seems mean, and life is hard enough without people throwing roadblocks in the way—like I did tonight with Eliana. Thanks for calling me out. Eliana should've phoned for an exorcist. Or maybe she did—are you a priest?"

Whitney laughed until she started to cry. "You really should write some of that down."

"That's what your grandmama said. She gave me a journal to write things in."

A strange look came over Whitney's face, but not like she was jealous. It was more like she was puzzling something out.

"Wanna see it?" I asked. I took the journal out of the bookshelf and noticed the book I'd shoved it in next to. "Son of a monkey! There *is* a book called *Lord of the Flies*!"

Whitney burst out laughing again. She checked out the journal, then she zeroed in on my assignment. The girl does stay focused.

"If the Higglby part bothers you, why not concentrate on your mother's family?"

Now there was an idea! I googled my mother's maiden name, Corbyn.

"It means 'dark-haired person'—that sure doesn't describe me." I glanced in the mirror at the red lobsteresque mess on my head. "And mine always looks like a dry sponge."

"Yeah, there's nothing worse than white-girl hair problems," Whitney moaned, then added, "If you hate it so much, why don't you straighten it out a little?"

"Is that what you do?" I asked.

"There you go being white again," she said with minor disgust. "Mine grows this way." She pulled at a strand of her silky black hair. "Grandmama is from Louisiana. There are a lot of French people there so she figures there's a Frenchman somewhere in our family tree."

"Well, I'm jealous of your French hair."

"Some of *my* friends are too. Traditional African American hair is hard to style. But my friend Trissa is great at it—maybe she can help you restyle yours."

That was a thought. I didn't want to go to Mom's hairstylist because someone might see me before I was ready to be seen. But right now, I had a tree to plant.

Whitney redrew the tree. Hers looked fantastic! I wrote in the three names on my dad's side that I knew. But my mom's branches sprouted made-up names like Major General Ebenezer Corbyn and Duchess Lilian Von Brandt. No one would check this stuff so close to the last day of school—I knew it, my teacher knew it, and my great-grandfather Jacques Beaumont would know it if he weren't imaginary.

"Finally, a family to be proud of." I turned to Whitney. "Want to do yours?"

Whitney's eyes turned a little sad. "I wish I could. Most Black folks in this country haven't got a clue. White people didn't waste much time recording our history. The Louisiana stuff is all I know—and *it* might not be true."

After that sunk in, I said, "It must suck sometimes to be surrounded by white people."

Whitney stared at the floor. "It can suck to be white and surrounded by white people…if they're jackasses."

Whitney knew something she wasn't telling me.

"Meaning…"

"Your friends aren't as friendly as you think."

"Meaning?" I said again. "Come on, spit it out."

"What were you doing last Saturday night?"

"Nothing…why?" I asked warily.

"Your little pony phonies had a party without you."

"How would you know?" I asked defiantly.

"Is one of your friends named Richardson?"

She was onto something. Valerie's last name was Richardson.

"They hired Grandmama last week for a postsurgical assist at their house."

I remembered my mom saying Val's mother had an appendectomy last week—although Mom suspected it was really Botox and a nose job.

"Your grandma shouldn't gossip," I lashed out.

"She only told me because it upset her after she met you."

"What did they say?"

Whitney hesitated. "If I tell you, you'll think *I'm* a gossip."

"Tell me," I said, clenching my teeth. "Or I'll…"

"What? Not turn in your assignment? Make me ride somewhere on a horse?"

Whitney looked in the eyes of a very desperate me and gave in. "They were making fun of you. Something about your other dad being a junk dealer or something. Does he sell drugs?"

"No, he collects actual junk…antique junk. What else did they say?"

"That's all she told me—but she didn't do it to be mean. And I don't want to be mean either. I just think I'd want to know if my friends were jerks."

"They aren't jerks! They just—"

"Had a party you weren't invited to and made fun of your family."

She had me there.

Mrs. Sheppard called up to Whitney from the bottom of the stairs. Whitney bit her lip and looked at me.

"I'm glad you told me," I said.

After she left, I slowly faced the truth. My friends weren't drifting away from me because they thought I was a baby. They were running away from me because I was a Higglby. They were old enough now to understand bigotry—and callous enough to embrace it.

I put my fictitious family tree in my backpack and went to bed. My last name may be Higglby, I thought as I cried myself to sleep…but theirs should be Beelzebub!

8
Hunk Help

The last few days of school, I ignored the Phony Ponies, as Whitney called them. I think they were glad. I also think it wasn't Whitney that Mrs. Sheppard thought needed a good friend—it was me.

It was time for some soul-searching. I had always admired Valerie's confidence, but now I saw it wasn't confidence—it was arrogance. I didn't want to be around that anymore. But I also didn't want to go through seventh grade sitting by myself at lunch.

So, what kind of friends *do* I want? Obviously, kids who think like me, and act like me, and love horses like me. In my school, that leaves...me.

With Mom on the injury list, I'd been going to the stable more often to keep Grace company. But next week, I'd be going to the farm for the summer. It's just across town, but summer is supposed to be *Dad Time*, and since this was the last summer I'd spend at the farm, I wanted to do it right. That meant more father time for him and less horse time for me.

But today was penciled in for Grace. I tried to get Whitney to come with me, but she was *not* interested. So I biked to Silver Saddles alone.

As I curried Grace's coat, I did more soul-searching. How come I've only had three friends my whole life? Maybe I don't like people that much. Maybe I like horses more than people—or maybe I just trust them more.

I gave Grace an apple. Then I gave one to Valerie's horse, Sheba, in the next stall. Sheba seems unflappable—exactly like I'd want to be if I were a horse…or me. I hate it that Val uses spurs when she rides. They're the flat kind used to direct a horse in a way less noticeable than flapping your legs and knees around, but I think she overdoes it.

I was taking Grace for a short trail ride when I noticed the Filly Phosphorescents practicing jumps in the arena. They were definitely working hard to beat us this year. Still, I stopped to admire the paint horse one of them rides. He's a charmer with a brilliant black-and-white coat. I think his name is Smokey. Some horses just draw your eye to them—Smokey and Grace both come to mind.

Then I realized someone next to me was also admiring the paint. It was Creamery Hunk! I hadn't seen him since my ill-fated jump. With any luck, he wouldn't recognize me.

"Hi, Grace's owner," he said smoothly.

Thanks for nothing, luck!

"Hi, Creee…" I stopped before saying Creamery Hunk.

"Close, it's Craig. What's your name?"

"Ki…Kathleen. I haven't seen you around lately."

"I haven't been…had a lot of final exams." He hoisted himself up on the fence. "I'm glad you didn't give up jumping after your fall."

"Actually, I did."

He stared at me with two very chocolate eyes. "You don't look like a quitter."

I decided to level with him, maybe because he was being so nice, or because he already knew the truth, or because looking into those eyes was like drinking truth serum.

"I just can't get over those stupid hurdles—at least not with a horse still under me. You saw me last time…I wet my pants."

Craig chuckled. "When I saw you go flying, I almost wet mine."

Now I laughed.

"You want to try it again?" he asked. "Grace needs a good workout."

My stomach began to churn. "You think she'd trust me?"

"The problem isn't your horse trusting you; it's you trusting your horse."

Craig hopped off the fence. "Let's give it a try."

We entered the arena. I didn't feel as scared as last time, maybe because it wasn't just the horse I decided to trust; it was Craig.

"Remember, she's the one jumping, not you," he said. "Just aim for the center of the jump and move with her rhythm. She knows when to jump. When you feel her taking off, lean forward, look straight ahead, and give her some rein. When she lands, follow her rhythm and you'll stay balanced."

I turned Grace toward the candy-cane jump and let Craig's words echo in my head: *She's the one jumping, not you. Move with her rhythm.* Grace broke into a canter and I rocked with her roll. Then I felt her go airborne. I leaned forward, slackened the rein, and before I knew it, she was on the other side slowing to a trot. And *I* was still in the saddle.

I looked at Craig. He shrugged like it was just that easy. And it was!

"Thanks for the lesson," I chirped. "I feel like I should pay you or something."

"No charge," he said with a smile. "I didn't do it for money. I did it because you remind me of my kid sister."

Bong! went a bell in my head. Like that poem says, *Ask not for whom the bell tolls*...it tolls for any girl who reminds a cute guy of his kid sister. I think part of me knew that all along, but a girl can dream! I guess there are worse things than a cute "big brother" who didn't treat me like a jerk.

I was ready to try another jump when I heard the unmistakable gaggle of voices known as the Pony Phonies. Craig heard them too.

"Gotta go," he muttered. "That group coming in is pretty high maintenance. I better get back to work."

I nodded. "Sorry they give you trouble."

Craig shrugged. "Nothing I can't handle."

With that, I left my first middle school crush behind and headed home knowing Grace and I had made a beautiful jump. That was almost better than a kiss...at least one from a big brother.

That night I picked up my new journal and opened it to the first gilded page. I took out the fancy pen decorated with

Egyptian hieroglyphics that was fastened inside the book and wrote "KIT CONCLUSIONS" at the top of the page. Then I wrote:

> It's fun to jump over a fence on a horse…more fun when you're still on the horse afterwards…most fun when someone you like is watching.
>
> ◊
>
> If you take the "r" out of Friends it spells Fiends!
>
> ◊
>
> It isn't easy to make up a family tree. Mine got an A for imagination, B+ for handwriting, and an F for research.
> Final Grade, C+.

9
The Prank

The last day of school was a half day. Eighth graders were excused after their graduation ceremony the night before, so I was roaming the half-empty schoolyard waiting for first bell when I saw Jonathan Rimroth crossing the campus.

You can't miss his silhouette—he's built like a drumstick. If you're unlucky enough to get closer, you'll also note the beady eyes, sweaty lip, and herringbone newsboy cap he likes to wear—possibly to cover the gentle slope of his forehead that suggests his brain might be missing. Before I knew it, the beast was upon me.

"Well, if it isn't Kit Kat, the junkyar—"

A soccer ball came flying across the yard and thwacked him on top of his head. Then, for an encore, the ball bounced straight up in the air, came back down, and bounced off his beetle-shaped skull again.

His first reaction was to see what poor fool accidentally hit him. *My* first reaction was to laugh—hey, it bounced off his head twice! Besides, if he'd been watching where he was going instead of taunting me, he would have seen it coming.

Never had first bell sounded more symphonic. It rang just in time to save me from another confrontation with the Butthead of Bully Town. But I should have known he'd remember my laugh longer than he'd remember the thwack.

When the last bell on the last day of sixth grade rang out *goodbye and good riddance*, I was ready to oblige. All I had to do was clean out my locker. Then I was going to meet Whitney at Trumble Middle School to see her mural Mrs. Sheppard had bragged about.

It surprised me to see Jonathan's sidekick, Bulldozer was still hanging around since eighth graders were dismissed. I began to wonder if he'd graduated.

The halls emptied fast. So fast that by the time I'd returned my guitar to the orchestra room, they were almost deserted. When I got to my locker, I could see my combination lock on the floor. The locker was empty. Everything was gone—my yearbook, my backpack, my mirror—everything except the dry-erase board. Someone had scrawled on it: "Your precious things are in Dumpster #2."

I sprinted to the back of the school. Two dumpsters were there. I ran to the second one and stood on tiptoe to look inside. It was only half full, so I could still see the top of my backpack gasping for air between lunch trash and heaven knows what else.

I hoisted myself up high enough to balance on the rim and tried to grab it. As I did, someone hurled me over the side of the dumpster into the trash. I lay there stunned, but I heard the loud pop of bubble gum right before the dumpster lid slammed shut, leaving me in darkness. Then I heard the muffled but unmistakable huh-huh-huh laugh of Jonathan Rimroth Jr.

Without the clues, I could have guessed it was him and his gum-popping pal. But at that moment, knowing who shoved me in wasn't as important as getting out. The smell was unrelenting—rotting meat, rotting sneakers, rotting rot. Even if I could get solid footing, I wasn't sure I could lift the heavy steel lid. My yells were falling on the deaf ears of an empty schoolyard on the last day of school. But yell I did!

Finally, I heard the squeaky lid of the dumpster being raised. I scrambled up to see Whitney's terrified face, followed by intense relief when I was the only thing that climbed out.

"I was afraid something with a hockey mask and chainsaw was in there!" she exclaimed.

"How did you find me?" I asked as my lungs groped for fresh air.

"When you didn't show up at Trumble, I came to see what was holding you up."

"I think it was old binders and a burrito grande," I said as I clawed my way out.

"What happened?"

"A guy named Jonathan Rimroth and his pet goon pushed me in. Rimroth's the head bully around here."

"Everyone in town knows that fool," Whitney said. "His dad is worse than he is. He owns the house we're living in. Nothing works and he won't fix it."

I pulled my backpack out of the dumpster and looked to see if anything else of mine was salvageable. All I could see were the photos I'd cherished of the Rein Bows...I left them there.

"You still want to see the mural?" Whitney asked.

"Unless you're ashamed to be with someone who smells like a crap sandwich."

"I'm good...unless the wind changes," she said.

We coasted into the Trumble parking lot and around to the back of the school. Then I skidded to a stop in front of a stunning mural painted on the side of the building—huge portraits of three people under the heading "H Is for Heroes."

"Know who they are?" Whitney asked. I shook my head.

"Helen Keller, Nathan Hale, and Harriet Beecher Stowe They all have a connection with Connecticut."

"Ah! Helen, Hale, and Harriet. Three Hs! What's that Latin gibberish at the bottom?"

"It's our state motto, doof. It's on the flag."

"Oh yeah. I've seen it, but I don't know what it means."

"*Qui transtulit sustinet.*" Whitney translated: "He who transplants continues to sustain."

"What did they transplant?"

"Themselves, I guess. The founders were colonists who settled here. But, as I recall, a few million enslaved people eventually got transplanted, too, along the way."

"What were they trying to sustain?" I needled her. Whitney pondered the question.

"I think the country is still wrestling with that problem," she answered. "But if whatever it is doesn't become rooted in moral dignity soon, I suspect it will end in chaos."

The answer stunned me. "Wow! Are you sure you're just a sixth grader?"

"I read a lot." She shrugged.

"Same question."

Whitney laughed and grabbed her bike while I stood there staring at the mural in awe. I couldn't believe someone just a few months older than I am could draw so beautifully. I felt proud to be standing next to her.

"I thought your grandma was just being a grandma, but you, Whitney Sheppard, are an artist!"

Whitney's smile filled her face.

"Are you coming over to the house?" I asked.

She nodded. "Dad's working late at the bakery, and Grandmama doesn't like me being home alone."

"I don't like to be home alone either. Wanna race?"

"Why? You know I'll win."

"Not if I can keep you downwind of me. I'm really starting to stink."

I pushed off and started for home while Whitney was still laughing.

10
The Shot

When Dad came to pick me up for the summer, I hadn't said goodbye to Mom yet, so he sat in the entryway to wait. I tried to picture him with Mom. There's no way they didn't make a cute couple. Dad still looks fit enough to knock a hole through an iron door. And he missed out on the Higglby hair. His is brown and wavy.

He sat, one leg crossed, the other jiggling a mile a minute. Not wanting to prolong his agony, I hurried into Mom's room. She was sitting up in bed, waiting to hand me a small velvet box. In it was a stunning gold Rolex watch with a rose-colored dial.

"Just a little something to remind you of me this summer. I know you have a clock in your phone, but that's a hassle… *this* is jewelry."

I loved it, which she knew because we had the same taste in jewelry. I reminded her I wasn't going to the moon—the farm was just across town.

"That farm is why I have another surprise for you," she said. "Mrs. Sheppard is going to give you a tetanus shot."

"Son of a monkey!" I was hoping she'd forgotten. Tetanus is sometimes called "lockjaw" because you can't open your mouth or swallow—which also happens when you're told you need a tetanus shot. They're one of the real ouchers.

I sat there dreading it while Mrs. Sheppard helped Mom into the bathtub. Then, while Mom was whirlpooling, Mrs. Sheppard went to work on me. I watched her remove the needle cap and pull back the plunger on the syringe. I stared at my arm, cringing at the thought of a needle going into it. Then Mrs. Sheppard paused.

"I'm glad you're here because there are two things I wanted to tell you." She looked around, then lowered her voice. "I was looking at the lady in that picture the other day." She nodded toward the painting on the wall—the one with the lady in the gold dress. "While I was looking at her, I swear I saw her wink. Have you ever seen that after you stare at her a few seconds?"

I stared at the lady with the big eyes to see if she would blink.

Then I heard Mrs. Sheppard say, "All done." And she was slapping a Band-Aid on my arm with a playful grin on her face.

"So, you never really saw that lady wink," I said accusingly.

"That's the second thing I wanted to tell you—don't believe everything you hear."

Zap! I laughed, then thanked her again for the journal. "I've already written in it."

"Oh, I'm so glad! That book seemed destined for greatness, and so do you."

I left the room feeling two feet taller and ten years smarter. I also left knowing that Mrs. Sheppard was one special person. But I didn't know that it would be the last time I ever saw her.

11
Busted!

Dad tossed my bike and suitcase in his pickup, and we were off to the Higglby farm. Mom hates the truck, but Dad's new wife, Angie, doesn't mind it. I saw her driving it last summer. I should've known then she was more than a friend. Dad doesn't let just anyone drive his truck.

I decided having Angie in the picture was a good thing for Dad. It would make it easier to spring Operation New Vacation on him. Dad broke the silence.

"Sorry to hear about your mom's accident. How's she doing?"

"Okay. She's got a day nurse, a night nurse, and a physical therapist working on her."

"Well, at least she's home," he said.

Dad isn't a fan of hospitals. His father died in a hospital when Dad was my age. That's when Dad started spending lots of time at the farm with his granddad—yes, the one everybody calls crazy. Good ol' Great-granddad to me.

"Hang gliding, huh? At least she's still got some spunk!" Dad chuckled.

That's one thing Mom and Dad had in common—*neither* of them ever grew up. If they were still married, they would've *both* been hang gliding. The difference is Dad wouldn't have crashed. He believes he can do anything he puts his mind to... and he usually succeeds.

Then he ambushed me. "I hear this is going to be our last summer together."

I'd told Mom about two parts of my three-part plan, but I didn't know she'd blab to *him*.

"No offense," I assured him. "But summer is the only time I can visit other places."

"I get that—my baby girl is growing up."

Once you leave the town limits, there are only two roads to the farm, and both go around the heavily wooded area everyone calls the Forbidden Forest. You can probably see all the yellow signs from space. They dot the property line every few yards: "Posted: No Trespassing" and "Trespassers Will Be Prosecuted. That means YOU!" One of them even has a skull and crossbones on it.

As we passed the Forbidden Forest, Dad blew the lid off of Operation Name Change.

"I hear you're going to change your name—which one?"

That threw me for a second. "Well, now that you mention it, both of them. I think Kathleen sounds more grown-up."

"First names are easy to change, but you'll always be a Higglby."

"I just don't want to advertise it. I'm tired of kids making fun of me—they make fun of you too."

"I know. Granddad didn't make it easy for me either with those stories of land mines and two-headed freaks. But changing my name wouldn't have helped; neither would blaming him. You've got to learn to kill your own snakes."

"How did *you* kill them?"

"I kicked their ass in football and baseball, on and off the field if need be." He glanced at me. "But there are other ways. What are you good at?"

It was easier to think of what I wasn't good at—studying, making friends, climbing out of trash cans…then I thought of something.

"I think I might like to write."

"Well, there you go! Next time someone makes fun of you, write 'em a note and pin it on their front door. Then while they're reading it, I'll run up and kick their ass!"

We both laughed. Then Dad said, "Here's the thing, Kitten, if it makes you happier to change your name, you should. But whatever you call yourself, you and I will always be Higglbys." A strange look came over his face. "I believe that's a good thing."

Did I just get a glimmer of "the look" Mom had told me about? I made a mental note to include an OPERATION INTERROGATION in my summer plans. Maybe Angie knew something about him being spooked by a tree.

Then Dad changed the subject again. He wasn't one to linger on topic.

"Did I tell you I'm starting a new business?"

Dad is always starting a new business. The last one was growing organic fruit, and, of course, there's his junk business where he drives around the country looking for old stuff people are trying to get rid of or sell cheap.

"There's a new bakery in town, and I've talked the owner into adding some other things to the menu. We're even building a new wing onto his store."

"My friend's dad works at a bakery," I mentioned.

"Last name Sheppard?"

I nodded.

"That's the guy. I'm driving into town later with some strawberries. Want to come?"

My dad was going into business with Whitney's dad? I definitely wanted to come.

We bounced up the dirt road past Lime Street on the other side of the Forbidden Forest. Finally, we ground to a halt in front of the farmhouse.

"I've got some must-do work outside," Dad said cheerily. "Why don't you unpack, then I'll give you the grand tour. Angie's been fixing up the house."

The place looked the same on the outside—old and creaky. When I was a kid, most of the rooms were kind of spooky. They were cold, neglected, and poorly furnished; the wind whistled and moaned through the shingles, and my poorly lit bedroom invited strange shadows to dance on the walls.

I knew Angie was the artsy-craftsy type, but I wasn't expecting to walk through the front door into a kaleidoscope!

The living room was ablaze in purple. The walls in the den, which I now call the Peacock Palace, were a pattern of turquoise, green, and royal blue.

I wheeled my luggage through a polka dot hallway and opened the door to my room. The wall behind my bed had been repainted with plain white paint. I didn't know whether to feel glad or neglected.

I tossed my backpack on the floor and flopped down on the bed. That's when I saw the only wall not painted white. It was covered with embossed wallpaper. The background was a pasture with a hint of flowers. And galloping through the pasture were three life-size horses. One was black, one was silver, and one was the chestnut color of Grace. The embossed paper gave everything a 3D effect, so the horses looked like they were galloping right out of the wall.

"Wow!" I said out loud to no one. Now I was doubly anxious to go into town. Angie was probably at the antique store, and this woman needed to be thanked—maybe applauded!

I ran outside to see if Dad was ready to go. Just past the backyard, I could see the infamous "junkyard" with the usual cast of characters: a wrought-iron colonial planter, the shell of a VW Beetle, and my new favorite—a cast-iron planter in the shape of a sleigh, Santa not included.

Dad loves his ever-changing pile of junk. He can buy an old sign or a set of toy trains faster than I can eat a Twizzler. He calls them "pieces of Americana." It shouldn't have surprised anyone that he'd move here when Great-granddad died. All Dad ever wanted was a junkyard to call his own.

Suddenly I heard a "Whooo-hah!" and Dad came out from behind a hedge, wearing a beekeeper hat and a big smile.

"Wanna taste some Grade A royal jelly?"

Since I didn't know what that was, I passed.

"You're a beekeeper now? Like people don't think we're crazy enough?" I grimaced.

"Should I start a rumor they're killer bees?"

"No!" I pleaded. "And why bees?"

"Partly because Ned uses honey instead of sugar in most of his bakery goods. And partly because he's been experimenting with a mead recipe I found in the kitchen after Granddad died. We're thinking of selling that too."

"What's mead?" I asked reluctantly.

"A drink made from fermented honey—kind of a weak beer."

"I didn't know Great-granddad drank."

"Neither did I. But he sure wrote down a good recipe."

I began to rethink Great-granddad. Maybe he hadn't taken a deep dive into Crazy Pond; maybe he was just drunk.

Dad kept prattling. "Our mead will run about five percent alcohol."

"My math is weak, but that doesn't sound like much."

"It isn't. Hell, cooking vanilla is thirty-five percent... can I say *hell* around you yet?"

"Only if you're sober."

"We're adding a room onto the bakery so we can sell mead and bitters. We're calling it Bitters 'N Sweets."

"And bitters are...?"

"Ancient Egyptians made them out of fruits and herbs and bark and stuff. And if it's good enough for King Tut, it's good enough for me. Ready for the grand tour of the farmhouse?"

Dad was like a billiard ball—he kept bouncing off the walls of life and eventually found a pocket. And thus, my guided tour began.

12
The Hidey-hole

Angie had turned the faded rooms into a modern museum. We went down Polka Dot Hall to Lotus Blossom Loft, then stopped off at the Panther Room.

She'd made that one into a trophy room for Dad—the name of his high school team being the Panthers. She had set out all his trophies and game balls and enlarged some of his high school pictures—although I didn't see one with Mom, his prom queen, prominently featured.

"Angie loves to decorate," Dad announced proudly. "I can't wait to see what she does with the hidey-hole."

"Hidey-hole?" I echoed.

"You've never seen the cellar?"

I shook my head. The house had always been spooky enough without *looking* for something scary. Dad grabbed a flashlight and opened the door to a musty room.

"This was part of the original house built in the 1700s," he explained. He threw back the edge of a ratty old rug, then pulled at a slightly raised board and swung it open.

I peered down in amazement. "A door in the floor? Why?"

"We think it was a root cellar and a place to hide in an Indian attack."

My eyes widened. "Were they ever attacked?"

"Don't know. But I wouldn't waste time building a place to hide if I wasn't expecting uninvited company. I've heard stories, but who knows if they're true."

"Why is it called a hidey-hole?"

Dad shrugged. "That's just what Granddad called it. He liked silly names. He didn't even mind being called Half-wit Higglby. I thought those were fightin' words until—"

Suddenly, Dad's mouth slammed shut like a prison door. This time I definitely saw the look—the one Mom must have seen. He went to some distant place in his head.

I tried to bring him back. "Are we going down there?"

Dad refocused. "It's a pretty tight fit for both of us. Why don't I go load the truck while you check it out?"

"Alone?" I squeaked.

"No guts, no glory," he said.

"I'm not worried about glory; I'm worried about spiders!"

"Oh, there might be spiders. Try not to scare 'em. They're pets." Then he left me to explore the hidey-hole alone.

My head said, Yikes! But the rest of me said, No guts, no glory! I grabbed the flashlight and hopped into the hole.

This dugout would be a tight fit for grown-ups. Still, if you're hiding from a disgruntled Mohican, I guess you don't need a lot of space to be scared stiff in. There was an old pot and some garden tools in one corner, but not much else.

I was about to declare this place uninhabitable *and* uninteresting when I heard a scratching noise. I swung the flash-light around and saw a mound of dirt move by the wall. Then I heard a scraping noise. A chipmunk peered up from the mound, then disappeared quickly.

No biggie. Chipmunks were all over the place out here—but what had caused the scraping sound? I grabbed a hand spade from the pile of tools and dug in the loose dirt. A few inches down, I hit something solid.

I scraped faster until I unearthed a small slab of wood. I pulled at the edge. It opened up like the trapdoor above me had. I was looking at a hidey-hole in a hidey-hole!

I trained the flashlight on it and peered in. I think my mouth fell open. Under the board in a stone compartment was an old metal box. I picked it up and opened the lid.

In the box was a beautiful pouch with beadwork and fringe. The pouch was tied with a complicated knot and had a note attached: "Do not open."

I drew my hand back. Something dangerous might be in there. Next to the pouch was a slip of paper with the name Hugo Higglby and the date 1785.

I wasn't sure what to do about all this. Should I show it to Dad? Would he open the pouch? *Should* he open the pouch? I put the box back in the hole for now. It had been there this long; it could wait a little longer. I needed time to think.

I replaced the board and pushed the dirt back over it.

13

New Stepmom

Whitney and I had been talking and texting, but I hadn't seen her since "dumpster day" at school—almost a week ago. She'd been working at her dad's bakery as his premier cake decorator. And with her ability to draw, I could see why.

As Dad and I rumbled down Main Street, I noticed Jonathan Rimroth's bike sitting at Izzy Burgers. His bike stands out because the tires have bright blue lettering on them. Fortunately, I didn't see him—making eye contact with that droid is like looking directly into a barf bag.

We pulled around to the back of the bakery where Ned Sheppard, Whitney's dad, came out to meet us. He was about Dad's height but had a stockier build.

"Where're my strawberries?" he demanded jokingly. "I've got pies to make."

"I just hope your pies deserve these berries," Dad retorted. "I may have to taste a few slices to ensure quality control."

"You've mooched enough off me," Mr. Sheppard snorted. "But I did sample one of our jugs of mead yesterday."

"How'd it taste?"

"Like floating on a cloud." Mr. Sheppard grinned. "But you be the judge. Come on."

I stepped out of my "invisibility" cloak. "Hi, I'm Kit. Is it okay if I say hi to Whitney?"

"Oh, I'm sorry," Mr. Sheppard said, noticing me for the first time. "Whitney isn't here. She's off somewhere with her friends."

That hit me like an iron fist. I wanted to say, "I thought *I* was one of her friends." But I just said, "Then I'll go over to the antique shop."

I grabbed my backpack and started down the block. I'd been planning to thank Angie for the fantastic wallpaper and maybe find out why Dad goes into those silent stares. But right now, I was trying to convince myself I wasn't being dissed again by a so-called friend. Whitney told me she was working today. Had she been working all those other days? I knew she had other friends, so why lie about it?

I looked up to see Antiques and Abandoned Treasure. Maybe *I* should open a business: Deceit and Abandoned Friendships—I have a few in my inventory.

Angie was finishing up a sale. I'd forgotten how energetic she was. Even when talking to tourists she'd never see again, she babbled like they were old friends.

When the customers left, she saw me and brightened even more.

"Kit! Max said you might come by today. How's everything going?"

"Great!" I lied, then thanked her for the incredible wallpaper. I could tell she was proud of it too. Then I remembered one more piece of business. I took the journal out of my backpack. "I'd like to put a lock on this in case I have friends over. You know how nosy they can be."

I was as likely to have friends over as I was to wrestle a potbellied pig, but I'd feel better knowing whatever I wrote would be seen by my eyes only. I remembered Mrs. Sheppard saying the journal would be a friend I could always talk to. At this moment, I wondered if it was the *only* friend I'd ever talk to.

"Oh, I remember this," Angie exclaimed as soon as she saw it. "I sold it to a lady who works at the hospital."

I nodded. "She thought it was a sketchbook."

"No, she asked for a journal," Angie assured me. "I showed her the lined pages."

Aha! I wasn't just an afterthought. Mrs. Sheppard had bought it especially for me, to help me through a tough time I was careening toward—being dumped by the Pony Phonies, and now, maybe her own granddaughter.

Angie snapped her fingers. "I have just the thing." She retreated to the backroom, then reemerged with some leather straps and a strange-looking combination lock.

She took out the pen fastened inside the journal. "This lock will go great with this pen's Egyptian hieroglyphic design. The lock has Egyptian combination symbols. Cool, huh?"

I agreed. The lock was antique gold and had five tiny combination wheels with hieroglyphs instead of numbers. Angie threaded the straps through the leather cover.

"Your friends will need a hedge trimmer to cut this off."

"Sold! How much?"

"Since you're family, no charge." She smiled.

That reminded me of Operation Interrogation. I dove in headfirst. "You mind if I ask you something about Dad?"

"Like what?"

"Does he ever act kind of, you know…strange?"

"You mean that silent stare thing?"

I nodded. Angie leaned over casually and propped her arms on the counter.

"I fell in *like* with Max because we shared the same passion for antiques. But I fell in *love* with him because he lets me be myself. I'm kinda quirky, and he's okay with that. I try to give the same space to him."

That was the end of *that* conversation.

I walked back to the bakery where Dad and Mr. Sheppard were finishing up their business. I heard Dad say he could probably find some outdoor chairs and tables cheap at an estate sale. Ned slapped him on the back like he was glad Dad had connections.

This time as we drove past Izzy Burgers, I saw Rimroth sitting outside with Dozer. I'm not sure if that annoyed me because they're both jerks or because he had more friends than I did.

I lay awake that night wrapped in total loneliness. Then I heard a text come in. It was from Whitney.

"U awake?"

I wanted to text back, "U are a horrible friend." But I just typed "yes." A few seconds later, the phone rang.

"Hi, Dad said you came by the shop today. Sorry I wasn't there."

"Me too—since you said you had to work today."

That brought a pause on the other end of the line.

"Are you mad at me?"

I didn't answer.

"It was a last-minute thing. There was a summer concert in Waterbury, and one of my friends wanted to go. Besides, it wasn't something you'd want to do."

"I wouldn't want to go to a summer concert?" I pouted.

"It was B Day Sway."

"What's that?"

"Exactly," Whitney answered. "He's a rapper Holly likes."

"Well, you still could've asked," I said, defending my hurt. "And you didn't because you made a stereotypical assumption about me just because I'm white."

There was another pause. I expected to hear a disconnect signal. Instead, I heard—

"You're right. I'm sorry."

I was so glad we were still friends I couldn't speak. But before I could explain that, Whitney said, "Would you feel better if I told you Trissa says she'll straighten your hair if you'll buy all the product?"

I think my eyes got big. "Really?"

"Really."

"Will I have to listen to rap music while she does it?"

Whitney laughed. "I can't make any promises."

"No problem. I'll be there."

Then we just talked. I told her about our dads going into business together. She was as surprised as I had been. She knew her dad was expanding the shop, but she didn't know my dad was his partner. After we hung up, I sunk back on the pillow thinking I'd sleep well. Only I didn't.

The first night in a different bed can always seem strange, but this one was a nightmare—for real! Kids were looking down at me while I was trapped in an underground hole. They were sing-songing the chant: *"Higg-l-by, Higg-l-by, Higg-l-by."* Then Rimroth's brassy voice rang out, *"Kit Kat, the junkyard rat, prowls through garbage like an alley cat."*

I woke with a start like I always did when I had that dream. Thanks to a strip of moonlight through the window, I quickly remembered where I was. But after my heart stopped leaping through my chest, I realized there was still something bothering me—that underground hole. The hidey-hole.

Who was Hugo Higglby? And what was in that pretty little pouch that was so important?

I really should tell Dad, I thought. Then I remembered that strange look on his face. Maybe telling him would weird him out again. I decided I had the whole summer to make up my mind.

Through the streak of moonlight, I could still see the fantastic wallpaper. This time I fell asleep dreaming about Grace and me galloping through clouds…I think on gossamer wings.

14
The Makeover

Today was the big day—Makeover Monday!

Unlike the old rambling Higglby farmhouse, the houses on this end of town where Whitney lived were newer, but they were crowded together on small lots. Whitney had the day off, so I arrived at her house with a backpack stuffed full of hair products, as instructed. Things I'd never heard of—heat protectant, infusion, flat iron, serum—the works!

I stepped into the small but tidy living room where the girl named Trissa was laying out her arsenal, ready to attack my hair. The first thing I noticed about Trissa wa*s her* hair. It looked more like Whitney's than mine.

"Are you sure you know how to straighten hair?" I asked.

Whitney and Trissa both laughed and Trissa handed me her phone. I scrolled through pictures of her wearing her natural hairstyle—thicker than my hair, but just as curly.

"Let's do this!" I said decisively.

I washed my hair, and as Trissa toweled it off, two more of Whitney's school friends, Holly and Branca, dropped by.

"You're doing white girls' hair now?" Holly asked.

"Why not? I'm thinking about being a hairstylist when I get older—unless I become an actress," Trissa explained.

Holly wore her hair short around her face with the back up in braids. I wondered about Branca's roots—not her hair, her actual roots. She looked more Hispanic than African American, but I wasn't sure if it was rude to ask. I decided to stick to hair conversation.

"Did you braid your hair yourself?" I asked Holly.

"Not these," Holly answered.

"I tried to do braids once," I continued, trying to fit in, "but just on my horse." Oh crap! Did she think I was comparing her hairdo to a horse?

The room got deathly quiet.

"She has a horse at that riding academy across town," Whitney said calmly. It hadn't occurred to me that "my horse" was what caused the silence.

Holly stared. "You own a horse? That officially makes you the richest white girl I know."

Trissa finished putting something on my hair and turned on the blow dryer. The added noise got me off the hook for the moment. I could hear Holly and Branca arguing over what music to listen to until Branca said something in a foreign language.

"Quit talking that stuff around me. You know I don't speak Spanish," Holly said.

"And you know that's not Spanish," Branca corrected for what must have been the thousandth time, judging by her tone.

Whitney filled me in. "Branca speaks Portuguese."

"It does sound a little like Spanish," I reported, having taken all of one semester in it.

Branca groaned.

"Don't get her started," Whitney said as she helped Trissa section off my hair. Then came the critical part. Trissa started smoothing out strands with the flat iron. I watched as she worked her magic.

After she flat-ironed my whole head, she styled in a few curls. I was dumbstruck at the transformation. I looked spectacular!

"Can I pay you something?" I asked, still glued to my new image in the mirror.

"Nah, I was just practicing. Besides, I wouldn't know what to charge."

"Maybe she can give you a horse," Branca suggested. They laughed, but I wasn't sure if it was *at* me or *with* me.

I left everything I'd bought, including the flat iron, with Trissa as payment and thanked her again. Then I waved to Whitney. "See you tomorrow."

"What's tomorrow?" Holly asked.

"I'm spending the night at Kit's house."

"You guys wanna come?" I added. "We can make it a sleepover party."

Holly considered this. "Might be fun. You live in one of those mansions in the hills? I've never seen the inside of one."

"I stay at my dad's farm in the summer," I explained.

"Shoulda known that," Holly announced. "Anyone who owns a horse is bound to have a farm. Where is it?"

"It's the Higglby farm," I said.

That was a bad time for the music to end. You could've heard someone cut butter.

"The Higglby farm?" Branca repeated. "Count me out. I've heard that place is haunted!"

"I've heard your head is haunted," Whitney retorted.

"Your dad is that crazy junk man?" Holly wailed.

"He isn't crazy," I snapped. "And it isn't junk. It's antiques."

"Never mind them," Whitney said. "*I'll* see you tomorrow."

I was a little teed off as I left. How dare they judge me! They want to come over if I'm at Wendom Hills, but not if I'm at my dad's? I'm the same person in both places.

As I rode through town, I decided I wasn't ready to go home yet. I wanted to show off my new hairdo to someone besides my dad. No one I knew was at Crandall's Creamery, but Crandall's wasn't far from the movie theater. Maybe if I took in a show, some kids would be around when it let out.

I sat through the movie, drinking a giant soda and wondering how I'd ended up with two groups of friends but wasn't particularly popular with either one. When I emerged from the theater, I was surprised at how dark it had grown. The wind had picked up, and the smell of rain was in the air.

Then I saw Johnathan Rimroth and Dozer standing within barfing distance. Wearing his favorite newsboy cap, Rimroth started toward me with that walk he must have practiced for years—part ogre, part praying mantis.

"Hey, Dozer, look what the alley cat did to her ugly head. Now it's even uglier!"

There may be people in this world who don't mind being called ugly. I am not one of them.

Right then, a major gust of wind whipped down the street. Jonathan's hat flew off and bounced along the ground toward me. With alley cat-like reflexes, I stuck my foot out to trap it, then picked it up.

"Oh, I'm sorry. Were you training your pet bulldog to retrieve? Here, fetch!" I Frisbeed the hat into the air. It tumbled and bounced and flew and bounced, then ended its journey under the wheel of a car.

"Oops." I cringed. It was a sincere utterance of regret, which Jonathan didn't deserve after his vicious dumpster prank, but I think I saw his nostrils flare.

"You're dumber than I thought," he spewed.

"Maybe I can smarten her up," Bulldozer snorted. He took a step toward me. "You know why they call me Bulldozer?"

"Because you're loud and like to play in the dirt?" I answered, making a quick calculation that neither Rimroth nor his Muscle-in-Chief would hit a girl in the middle of the day in the middle of town.

I was right. Bulldozer never laid a hand on me. My bike, however, wasn't so lucky. He shoved his foot through the spokes. I grabbed my phone, but before I could talk, text, or tango, Rimroth knocked it to the ground and stepped on it.

"Oops!" he said, mocking me. "Have a nice walk home, freak!"

As they strutted into the theater, I yelled a few choice words at the two thugs, but the wind blew them back in my face where only my ears could hear them. It was probably just as well.

15

Through the Knothole

The bike's wheels were barely rolling, but I thought it could get me home. It rattled and bumped as I willed it to keep moving, but at the edge of town, it gave up the ghost.

I got off and dragged the bike along until I reached the dirt road. That's when the heavens opened up like a fire hose. In seconds, I was drenched with rain. And so was my beautiful hair…my new straight hair that no one got to see except Jonathan Rimroth.

My face was full of rain, my arms were full of bike, and my bladder was full of soda when I finally saw the "No Trespassing" sign with the skull and crossbones. I made a snap decision. I'd take a shortcut through the Forbidden Forest!

My arms were two aching noodles by the time I reached the woods. The trees gave some shelter from the wind and rain, but I hadn't planned on the darkness. Forests are nature's original sunblock, but with thunderclouds blanketing the sky, it was way spookier—and way more confusing.

Before I could say, "Holy crap! I'm lost in the woods!" I was lost in the woods. I realized the shortcut was a bad idea—and I hadn't even hit a land mine yet. I decided to ditch the bike. Then maybe I could get through this perilous patch of timber before it knew I was there.

I stashed my bike next to a huge, funny-shaped rock to make it easy to find. Then I started in the direction I hoped was out of the woods and toward the house.

Suddenly, a flash of lightning lit up the forest. Tree branches began to groan, crackle, and break. Then a blood-curdling scream filled the air, followed by a thud.

Had one of the heads of the two-headed man blown off? It was time to run. I took off but slipped in the mud and skidded to a stop next to a tree stump. Someone yelled again. But this time, it sounded like they were yelling for help.

Instead of sitting like a stump next to a stump, I inched my way toward the muffled sound. Then, right in front of me, I saw someone. A human, I'm hoping. His head was stuck in the knothole of a tree. Only one head, I'm hoping.

Part of me wanted to run, but the other part grabbed him by his waist to pull him out. After a mighty heave, his head popped out of the knothole and we both went sprawling onto the ground.

That's when we saw each other face-to-face. I was staring at a green-eyed boy with a spongy patch of frizzy red hair exactly like mine!

I sat stunned at how much this kid looked like me. But it didn't shock him at all.

"You blew out of the tree too, huh?" he said. Then he jumped to his feet. "Come on, kid, we better get back. You know the rules—if something happens to us outside, we're done for."

"Outside what?" I said in a voice an octave higher than soprano.

"The tree, of course. I must've had the gumption knocked out of me when I hit the ground. Otherwise, I wouldn't have mistaken an ash tree for our oak."

He looked around to get his bearings, then squinted at something behind me. "What in Polly's pudding is that?"

The kid who was calling *me* kid looked about sixteen. But he had the eyes of a green eyed hawk. What he'd spotted was my bicycle. He crossed to it.

"This thing yours?"

The outside of my head nodded, but the inside was sputtering, *What tree?* And, *Who is this guy?* And, *Would this be a bad time to wet my pants again?*

I blurted out, "It's my bicycle."

"It looks busted, but I know who can fix it." He hoisted the bike on his shoulder, looked around, and mumbled, "I'm quite bad at directions."

With that encouraging news, he started walking into a heavier part of the woods. I don't know if it was his friendliness, or because he had my bike, or because I didn't want to be left alone, but following him seemed like my best option.

As we walked, the wind died down and the rain let up. I noticed the boy was wearing strange clothes, but I couldn't put my finger on what made them seem so weird. He shifted my bike to his other shoulder.

"I'm Fief, by the way."

"Fief?" I repeated.

"Yeah—rhymes with thief."

I stared at him. "Are you one?"

"Of course not," he said indignantly. "That's just what I rhyme with."

"You might want to go with 'chief' or 'leaf' when you're introducing yourself to strangers," I suggested.

"Why? I'm not those things either."

He had a point, I guess. All I knew was another parent somewhere didn't know how to name a child.

Then this Fief guy said, "Which Higglby are you?"

I gulped. "How do you know my name?"

"Look at you! Who else would you be? Are you sure you don't know where our tree is?"

"*Our* tree?" I repeated.

He looked me over more carefully. "What did you say you call yourself?"

"I didn't. But if you must know, it's Kit."

Just then, a crack of thunder split the air so loud we both ducked. And that was just the first act. Suddenly, the sky was a pitcher of water and the Forbidden Forest was a glass.

"Aw, for the love of fiddlesticks!" Fief yelped. "It's got to be around here somewhere. A Higglby never falls far from it."

I began to hear distant voices like I was outside a crowded stadium. I told myself it was just the sound of the rain. But the closer I got, the more I could swear it was voices. Then, as suddenly as the downpour had started, it stopped.

That's when I looked up and saw the most awesome tree I'd ever seen! Its brilliant leaves were shimmering with raindrops. Its branches stretched so high that the top of the tree was out of sight. The trunk was massive! And you won't believe this—it had grown into the shape of an H.

My mouth was so wide open, if it had still been raining, I would have drowned. "Is that it?" I asked feebly.

"You're a Higglby, right enough. Only a Higglby can see the Higglby Family Tree."

I tried to slow my brain down so it could explain what I was seeing, but it didn't slow down. And neither did my mouth.

"Are you telling me you're a Higglby, and you live in this tree?"

Fief stared at me like I was the densest person he'd ever met. "Of course I do. We all do. Every Higglby who's ever lived!"

Then I saw his eyes lock onto something behind me. I heard a serious rustling of leaves and turned to see a coyote standing motionless.

"Better get inside," Fief warned.

"Coyotes are more afraid of us than we are of them," I said, trying to sound wise.

"Tell that to the skunk!"

That's when I saw a very nervous skunk between the coyote and us. Fief shoved my bike through a big knothole in the tree and disappeared inside.

I edged closer to the tree, wondering if the trunk was hollow enough to fit two kids and a bicycle inside. The skunk turned and lifted its tail.

Enough thinking. I dove headfirst through the knothole.

The Higglby Tree

I expected to find myself in a dark, bug-infested hollow tree. Instead, I was sprawled on the dirt floor of a round room. I blinked. The wood on the inside of the trunk was polished. I blinked again. I was definitely inside a tree. And so was my bike. And so was this kid, Fief.

Then, out of a gray mist floating above us like a fuzzy ceiling, a giant head as round as a snow globe poked through. The head was wearing a metal helmet shaped like a bowl.

"Who goes there?" he yelled in a husky voice. He saw Fief. "Oh, it's you."

A ladder descended from the mist, and Helmet Head climbed down carrying a lantern. He was stocky all over—even his leathery skin seemed to have an extra layer of bulk. He was wearing a tunic belted at the waist, with an ax on one side and a sword on the other.

When he reached the ground, he saw me sprawled on the floor, so he leaned over and poked me with a stick, which I thought was a little rude.

"A new Higglby, eh? What do you call yourself?"

"She says her name is Kit," Fief offered.

"Kit? What kind of a name is that?"

"It's my kind of name," I said defensively. "And who exactly are you?"

"You'll know me soon enough!" Helmet Head stood up to his full height and announced himself in a booming voice. "I'm Peerless the Plunderer."

Fief scoffed. "He *used* to be Peerless the Plunderer. Now he's Peerless the Doorman."

"That's an important job too!" Peerless shot back. He jangled a hefty set of keys dangling from his belt. "Keeper of the keys, I am."

"Are you the one who can fix my bike?"

Peerless raised one of his furry eyebrows. "That depends. What's a bike?"

"It's that thing there, stupid," Fief said, pointing to mine. "Except it's supposed to roll." Then to me, he added, "He's not the one. It's the professor I was meaning. I might could fix it myself, but I've got a lot of work to do, especially after this wicked storm."

He must be a forest ranger, I thought. "Where do you work?" I asked.

"Here in the tree, of course. I'm one of the most important Higglbys here! I have a *useful* skill," he said pointedly to Peerless. "I was a carpenter's apprentice in the World, so they put me in charge of tree branch repair."

"In the World?" I echoed.

"Yeah, before I came to the tree."

These guys must be joking around, but I played along. "How long have you lived here?"

Fief counted it off on his fingers. "Two hundred fifty years, give or take."

I rolled my eyes. "No one can live that long."

Fief rolled *his* eyes. "I know that! I'm only fifteen years old. It's two hundred fifty years I've been dead."

"Oh, I didn't realize you were dead," I said sarcastically.

Fief got that look older kids get when they're tired of explaining stuff to younger kids. "Of course I'm dead. We all are. Even you!"

That was not funny.

"Look, I don't know who you guys are or how you know my name, but I'm not dead. See?" I started jumping around, waving my hands and stomping my feet until I bumped against the wall of the tree and knocked myself flat—again.

Peerless chuckled. "She's a Higglby, right enough. Too bad, though. A Higglby dead at such a young age."

"I am not dead!" I said, scrambling to my feet.

Peerless the Plunderer leaned down like a teacher getting ready to shake his finger in my face—a gesture I'm familiar with. "You a Higglby?" he asked gruffly.

"Yes."

"You can see this tree?"

"Yes."

"Then you're dead."

I'd heard enough. All I wanted was to get out of there.

I turned and dove headfirst out of the knothole and landed back in the Forbidden Forest. I ran in what I hoped was the direction of the farmhouse. But frankly, I didn't care where I was going as long as it was away from that tree!

After several terrifying minutes, I finally saw a patch of light through the endless swirl of trees. My eyes were so locked onto that clearing I ran smack into something metal. I staggered backward wondering what new disaster had presented itself. It was the back of the "No Trespassing" sign on Lime Street. I flew past it running straight for the house.

I couldn't blot out that terrible thought. Maybe I *was* dead. Maybe that lightning strike came closer than I thought—a lot closer!

I blasted into the house and headed straight for a big mirror I'd seen in the Purple Room. I stared into the mirror and saw my reflection staring back. Relief rushed through me. I wasn't dead because I could see my reflection—or was that just vampires… or werewolves? I couldn't remember.

Then I heard a glorious sound—Dad's truck pulling into the drive. When he opened the front door, I almost tackled him.

"C-can you see me?"

"See you what?" he asked. Then he saw the muddy floor. "I can see you should've left those shoes outside! We don't have a housekeeper around here, young lady. You mess it up; you clean it up."

That was music to my ears. I must be alive! Surely, kids don't get chewed out for tracking in mud if they're dead.

Then Dad's face froze. He stared at me staring back at him.

"You saw it," he said. "You saw the tree."

I nodded.

"You think it's really there?"

"I know it is. I was inside of it."

His eyes widened. We sat down in the kitchen, and Dad started talking.

For the first time, he shared his secret of the day he'd gone to the forest to get firewood. He'd looked up and thought he saw an enormous tree, but it was faint—like seeing it through a blurry lens. He took a few steps closer, but something stopped him.

"You mean someone?" I asked.

Dad shook his head. "It was more like a force—like a magnet repelling me. Then the tree disappeared."

"Did you tell Great-granddad?"

"I was afraid to tell anyone. I knew they'd think I was just another crazy Higglby. But the night Granddad died, he told me he'd seen it too. Like me, he only saw it once, and he couldn't approach it. That was why he put up those no-trespassing signs and started telling stories about land mines and monsters being in there. Whatever was there, he wanted it left alone."

Suddenly I saw crazy Great-granddad Higglby in a whole new light. He wasn't a maniac; he was a guard…a sheepdog protecting a mystical flock.

Dad now looked at *me* in a whole new light.

"Can you take me there?" he asked suddenly.

"I can try, but I'm not sure where I was. It was pouring rain and I—"

"We have to look, Kitten. I think it's our tree. I think it's the Higglby Family Tree."

17
No Guts, No Glory

What Dad said added up to what I had seen: the kid wearing old-fashioned clothes, the Viking guy, them knowing my name and saying I must be dead if I'm in the tree.

But I wasn't dead, so why was I there? Why didn't the same force that stopped Dad and Great-granddad stop me?

Part of me never wanted to go there again. But the rest of me knew I didn't want to spend my life wondering what it was or *if* it was. Besides, I'd promised Dad I'd take him there—if I could figure out where "there" was.

I decided not to go back empty-handed. The next morning, I went down to the hidey-hole's hidey-hole and took out the metal box. If a Higglby left it there, he must be in that tree. I stuffed the box in my backpack and met Dad at the back door.

We entered by the "No Trespassing" sign that had almost flattened me the day before, and it wasn't long before Dad spotted my sneaker tracks. Then I recognized the big rock where I'd ditched my bike. My bike! I just remembered—it was still in the tree.

Any thoughts that I'd somehow imagined it melted away for good. Then I saw it! The magnificent tree with a trunk in the shape of a swirly H.

"There it is!" I whispered to Dad. "Can you see it?"

He shook his head. "No. All I see is a kind of haze, but I can sure feel it. It won't let me get much closer."

I didn't feel anything. "I'll take a look," I said.

Dad pulled me back. He'd waited most of his life to find the tree again, but now he was afraid for me.

"Are you sure?" he asked.

"No guts, no glory," I said with more courage than I felt.

I walked to the tree and listened for voices. It was quiet as a tomb—maybe a poor choice of words. I stuck my arm through the knothole then pulled it out to test if I could go in and out when I wanted. I stuck my head in. The little room was there, but it was empty.

I turned and gave Dad a thumbs-up and glanced at my watch. It was nine o'clock.

To test the knothole one more time, I stuck my head in the tree. Before I could pull it out, a heavy hand came down on my neck and pulled me inside. The hand belonged to Peerless the Plunderer.

"Oh, it's you." He let go of my neck and bit off a chunk of black goo he was holding.

"What's that?" I asked, deciding small talk was the way to go.

"Tree tar. Nothing better to eat—except maybe rat-on-a-stick." He popped the rest of the tarball in his mouth. "You're lucky, missy. Lots of them that leaves the tree never come back."

"I won't be staying," I said timidly, hoping he wouldn't be offended. He wasn't.

"Fine with me," he belched. He sauntered over to the ladder hanging from the mist where a ceiling should be.

His lack of interest in whether I stayed or went was a relief. But when he started up the ladder, I blurted out, "I need to see Fief."

"So go see him."

"I don't know my way around," I protested. "I…I've only been dead a couple of days."

I creeped myself out saying that, but Peerless kept climbing, so I kept talking. "Could you take me to him? You must know this tree better than anyone."

Peerless puffed out his already puffy chest. "That's true," he said proudly.

I made a mental note that Peerless the Plunderer was also Peerless the Easily Flattered. Good to know. He paused in mid-climb to think. Something told me walking and thinking at the same time wasn't something Peerless did easily.

"Fief, eh? He's probably with the professor." He rubbed his lower back. "I'll take you this time, but I've been getting the back grabs lately, so after this, you're on your own."

He started climbing again, then noticed I wasn't following. "Well, what are you waiting for?" he bellowed.

"I—I'm a little scared." My voice was so shaky it surprised even me.

"Scared of a tree? *Your* tree?" He shook his head. "Good Gotliep! This family went downhill fast!"

I gathered my courage and started up the ladder behind him.

"Is Fief related to the professor?"

"Nephew, I think. He was a carpenter's apprentice until that war. He calls it the American Revolution."

"Fief fought in the Revolutionary War?"

"Not exactly—he took a musket ball in the chest on his way to join up. Bad luck his whole life, that one. He can't even find his parents."

At the top of the ladder was an upper floor where a rickety old elevator stood. We walked in, and Peerless clanged the door shut. He moved the lever on a clunky wheel and watched a pointer slowly swing past numbers scrawled above the elevator door. The first one we passed was 21.

"Them's the century," he explained.

When we got to 19, the elevator jolted to a stop and Peerless opened the door. Outside the elevator was a large wooden door. Peerless located a key on his big brass ring of keys and shoved it into the lock.

"Why all the locks? Can't we go where we want in our own tree?"

Peerless shook his head. "Not anymore. After a millennium, we started locking the main door to each century to keep the riffraff from causing mischief."

"Riffraff?"

"Higglbys by marriage only. When Higglbys who ain't blood relatives die, they go to their own trees. Husbands and wives and the like can only stay or visit if they're on the list. That's where I come in. I'm also Keeper of the List."

Peerless opened the door to a long, winding hallway. Other numbered hallways branched off from it. If I understood the system, each number represented a different year in the nineteenth century. We walked some more.

"If all Higglbys live in this tree, why can't Fief find his parents?"

"It's a big tree. It goes all the way across the ocean, and the lad's got no sense of direction."

Peerless halted and pounded his meaty fist against a door until a wrinkly-headed man swung the door open. Peerless looked surprised.

"Lye Water Willy? What did you do with the professor?"

"He's two doors down, you bungling bag of pusillanimity! Now go away! I'm making soap!" He slammed the door shut.

"Someday I'll give him the back of my ax, that himthicky!" Peerless muttered.

I have no idea what pusillanimity or himthicky mean, but I doubt you'll find either word on a piece of valentine candy.

Two doors down, Peerless knocked again. This time, Fief opened the door.

"Kit? Your bike isn't ready yet. But don't worry, the professor will figure it out. He knows everything!"

Meeting a Higglby in this tree who knows *anything* would be a novelty, I thought. But I was about to be surprised.

18
The Mad Scientist

I suddenly remembered my hidey-hole box and handed it to Fief. "I think this belongs to someone here. Do you know a Hugo Higglby around year 1785?"

Fief looked surprised. "I do! We got here about the same time. You want I should give it to him?"

I hesitated, then decided it belonged more to the tree than to me. I handed it to Fief, then turned my attention to an old man busy at work with a blowtorch. He had a gray blob of Higglby hair on top of his head with frizzy strands shooting out in all directions.

When the old man looked up, there was no doubt about it—the eyes staring through thick wire-rimmed glasses were the marble-green eyes of a Higglby.

"What's your name again?" he asked me.

"Kit Higglby, what's yours?"

"Professor Elbert Faraday Higglby."

"He's a genius," Fief bragged. "The greatest mind the Higglby family has ever known."

If he was such a genius, I wondered why he hadn't fixed my bike yet.

"Still repairing your two-wheeler," Elbert said like he'd read my mind.

I saw a big lump of molten metal on the table. Then I recognized it. It was my bike! Or what *used* to be my bike. The professor had taken a blowtorch to it.

Fief was beaming. "Uncle Elbert's got quite a brain. He invented the Theory of Higglby Branchitivity. Everything we know about our tree and how it works we learned from him."

Hearing this man was the family genius was disheartening. I decided to test his "genius" label. "So what *is* the Theory of Branchitivity?"

The professor tapped a chalkboard with the blowtorch. On the board was the drawing of a tree with countless branches, numbers, and weird-looking symbols splattered around.

"Family trees have been growing since the beginning of human existence," the professor began. "When a person dies, the body transubstantiates and enters their tree, which only deceased members of said family can see or enter. The main branches constitute the centuries; smaller branches, the different generations. Thus, the tree grows ad infinitum!"

The professor drew the mathematical symbol for infinity on the board with a piece of chalk. "However," he added pointedly, "outside this tree are universes where life in that century is still going on. But anyone who ventures outside the tree is no longer protected by the construct of the tree. If anything happens to them, their tree bodies disappear forever!"

"Forever?" I repeated.

"Forever in their human form. They become particles in the universe. Nothing can die twice in its exact same form. There is molecular disintegration. If something happens to our immortal forms when we are outside the tree, another transubstantiation occurs and we—phhht!—disappear.

"I have also found that those who venture outside the tree cannot change history to any great extent. That would be like trying to put toothpaste back in the tube."

"What's toothpaste?" Peerless asked.

The professor waved his hand as if to say "later" and continued his theory. "A murderous act by a tree denizen, for instance, causes that universe to split off and form another one, again, from which you cannot return."

Elbert Faraday Higglby folded his arms and stared down at me. "Understand, little girl?"

I nodded. "Except your theory has a hole in it."

Fief froze. Peerless gasped. The professor scoffed.

"Show me where!" he demanded.

I pointed to myself. "Right here. I can see the tree and enter the tree, but I'm not dead."

"Of course you're dead," he muttered. "I'll prove it."

He rummaged through his desk and pulled out something that looked a little like a stethoscope that doctors use.

"When a person dies, the soul takes the form of your original body and comes to the family tree. Ergo, the soul is no longer *in* you. It is now all of you. This souloscope proves the theory."

The professor hooked something to a monitor. A flat line appeared on the screen. Elbert put the souloscope against Fief's heart and spoke into the other end.

"Hello?" Elbert said. He smiled at me. "See? No reply."

He crossed to Peerless, who had plopped down on an oversized couch and was polishing his helmet. Elbert put the scope to Peerless's chest. "Hello?" No answer.

Elbert turned to me. My heart was pounding like a jackhammer. I sure knew *it* was present. The professor put his souloscope against my chest.

"Hello?" he said into it. My voice came out of the machine as the flat line began to dance.

"Hello, yourself," I heard my voice say, but my lips weren't moving. Elbert's eyes almost popped their sockets. He spoke into his souloscope again.

"You're still in there?" he asked in amazement.

The machine line twitched up and down. "Of course! Where else would I be?"

The professor lowered the souloscope. "My dear, I believe you are, indeed, alive!"

I was elated, but Peerless had a different reaction.

"There's a mortal in the tree?" He jumped up and pulled out his ax. "Let's kill her!"

"Put that away," Fief said, stepping between Peerless and me. Peerless stuffed his ax back in his belt.

The professor stared at me. "You must be the product of a genetic mutation."

Peerless pulled his ax back out. "Let's kill her!"

Fief leveled him a stare. "Is that your answer to everything?"

"It's one of 'em," Peerless growled.

"Fief is right," the professor scolded. "Something different sometimes turns out to be a treasure."

"Then let's bury her!" Peerless shouted and glared at Fief. "That's my other answer to everything."

Elbert shook his head. "Not all treasures should be buried, my boy. Some should be protected and admired."

Peerless thought, then yelled, "Let's make her our queen!" He knelt down in front of me and bowed his head.

Between hearing my soul talk, having an ax waved in my face, and being anointed queen, I was ready to call it a day. "Uh, about the bike—I'll come back for it later."

Fief grinned. "We await your return, Your Majesty." He doffed his cap and bowed.

Frankly, I wasn't making any plans to return. Having just proven the smartest man in the family wrong, I spun around and walked gracefully past the kneeling Peerless—until I tripped on his sword and careened into a bookshelf, knocking some books onto the floor.

"Too clumsy to be *my* queen!" Peerless yelled. He tried to rise from his kneeling position, then grabbed his back and cursed a blue streak, I think. He definitely wasn't singing a lullaby.

"Confound it! I fear I need one of your poultices, Professor. It's the only thing that eases my back grabs."

"Sorry, Plunderer, but I'm out of most of the ingredients."

While the professor scribbled some items on a list, Fief explained to me that a poultice was herbs and spices mixed together to relieve pain.

The professor handed Peerless the list. "I'll need these things. But of course, you'll have to go outside to find them."

I assumed "outside" meant outside the tree—especially when I saw Peerless's ruddy face turn pale.

"I can't leave the tree. I'm Keeper of the Keys!"

"You're scared is what you are," Fief teased. "No one calls you Peerless the Fearless."

Peerless struggled to his feet. "I fear no man nor beast... unless it's trying to disappear me forever!" He grabbed the paper from the professor and shoved it in his belt.

I started to pick the books up I had dislodged, but Elbert waved us away.

"Be off now. I have work to do—except you," he said to Fief. "I may need help with this bi-wheeler."

Peerless and I trudged back down the hall and into the elevator. When it stopped with a thud on the lobby floor, he opened the door.

"Since you're still counted among the living, don't make no plans for coming back here 'til you ain't," he said stiffly.

"But I'm a Higglby," I protested.

"Not a tree Higglby," Peerless countered.

I didn't argue the point. I was more concerned with getting back to Dad in case he was freaking out about me. But when I emerged from the tree, my dad looked startled.

"Back already?"

Already? I glanced at my watch to see how long I'd left him waiting. Whoa! It still said nine o'clock. Could an expensive new watch already be broken? I grabbed Dad's wrist and looked at his watch. It also said nine o'clock!

19

Tree Begone

"So what was in there?" Dad asked eagerly. "You just kind of disappeared into the haze."

"For starters, I think time stands still once you enter the tree. I was gone at least an hour."

"That kind of makes sense," Dad said slowly. "What would they need time for?"

He had a point. My mind was spinning. I had discovered a place that reached wherever Higglbys had ever been in the world. And in this mystical tree, time stood still!

On the way home, I told Dad what the professor said about Tree Branchitivity and parallel universes outside the tree—and how tree denizens killed outside the tree disappear forever.

When we got home, Dad made two cheese sandwiches, and we ate in silence at the kitchen table.

Then it had to be said, so I said it. "What do we do now?"

Dad took a sip of coffee, then looked me in the eye. "We need to forget about that tree."

"But—"

He held up his hand. "No buts. Just the vague sight of that tree haunted Granddad most of his life and most of mine. Hell, it cost me my marriage…and time with you."

I got a little sick inside but kept quiet.

"We still have our lives to live, Kitten. Whatever is in those woods doesn't belong to us yet. And if you tell what you saw, every person you know will think you're insane."

Dad was right. That tree was for the dead. Mutation or no mutation, living people had no business in that tree.

Unfortunately, I still didn't have a bike. Mom would've bought me a new one, but Dad offered to fix up one he'd found, so why hurt his feelings?

He was working on it the next morning in what used to be the barn. He'd remodeled it into a workshop-slash-museum. The museum part was where he kept his indoor junk.

It was cool how Dad decorated the walls with signs that used to hang in diners or roadside shops. Shelves dotted the room, filled with old lanterns, antique toys, and hand-painted jars. He spent hours out here repairing and polishing stuff.

But today, he was refurbishing the bike. He'd tightened the brakes, changed the bearings, and cleaned the chain. It was almost ready to go.

"You sure have a lot of stuff in here," I said, checking out an old rocking chair with hand-carved wooden slats.

"You see stuff. I see stories," Dad said. "Like that canteen over there. It's from Antietam—a Civil War battlefield. History isn't just names and dates. It's people's lives."

He nodded toward the rocking chair. "Someone's mother spent hours in that chair singing to a newborn baby. Some father told war stories or planned his tomorrows sitting there."

His eyes roved over the signs on the wall: "Route 66"; "Boots & Saddle Motel"; "Hot Rod Garage."

"These things tell the story of this country," he said proudly.

"How come you don't have any old coins?"

He shrugged. "I like collecting things people treasure more than treasure people collect."

Every day my dad seemed smarter to me.

That afternoon, I rode Dad's bike to the stables. I was as glad to see Grace as she was to see me. When I spotted Craig, I explained I was at my dad's for the summer, so I wouldn't be around as much.

Craig had spent extra time with Grace since Mom was still out of commission. "I've been taking her through jumps like ones for the quarterfinals next week," he said. "She's a natural jumper. You should enter."

"No way!" I protested. I knew my limitations.

Grace and I rode around, then I fed her and mucked out her stable—that means "swept up poop." Then I went by the house to see Mom.

She was better. But when I asked what she was doing, she said she was waiting for her new nurse to arrive.

"New nurse? Where's Mrs. Sheppard?"

"Oh," Mom answered. "Didn't you hear? Mrs. Sheppard passed away."

20
The Cherrywood Box

I still felt like I'd been punched in the stomach when Whitney opened her front door.

"I just found out" was all I could say.

She nodded and invited me in. Holly and Trissa were gathering their things to leave when Whitney's cell phone rang.

"I have to take this," she said and left the room.

"I hope you aren't leaving because of me," I said to Holly and Trissa.

Trissa shook her head. "We've been here all morning. We were on our way out." She stared at my frizzy hair. "Didn't anyone like your hair?"

I didn't feel like going into how nobody even saw it—nobody I liked, anyway.

"It's a long story, I'll tell you later—but I'd love for you to fix it again. And this time, it will be a professional appointment."

Trissa smiled. Then Holly spoke up.

"I hope we didn't seem rude last time you were here. We didn't know you. But Whitney says you're okay. And if she says you're all right, you're all right."

I'm not much of a hugger, but I felt like hugging both of them. So I did.

After Holly and Trissa left, I gazed around the room. The last time I was here, I hadn't really noticed anything but my hair. This time I took in the homey feel—a Grandmama Sheppard feel. Everything seemed to fit. That's what pulled the room together—the feeling that everything belonged.

There were three framed photos on the mantel. One was Grandmama Sheppard in her hospital scrubs; one was her wearing an African head wrap; one was her in a wedding gown. In each picture were the unforgettable eyes and ever-present smile. I heard Whitney returning.

"Thanks for coming by. There've been so many people here these last few days, Dad and I were a little overwhelmed. But he went back to work today. He said we have to keep putting one foot in front of the other."

"I'm glad you haven't been alone, but I wish I'd known. I wish…was there a funeral?"

That's when Whitney broke into tears.

"Just a memorial service so her friends could say goodbye," she sobbed. Her eyes moved to a cherrywood box on the mantle. "She wanted to be cremated. She used to say that we have to take up space on the planet when we're alive, but we shouldn't hog it after we're gone."

I never felt so helpless. I didn't know what to say to stop Whitney from crying—or if I should. Whitney looked back at the cherrywood box.

"It's called a keepsake chest. Ashes to ashes and dust to dust, that's what Dad says." Tears streamed down her cheeks. "I just can't believe that's all that's left…"

And that's when I blurted out, "That *isn't* all that's left! She's just gone to her tree!"

Oh god, I said that out loud! I didn't know which of us was more shocked. I looked to see if Whitney was giving me the "How crazy are you?" look. Yep, there it was. But it was too late to stop now. The rest came gushing out like water from a broken water main.

"It's true, I've seen it—and if you don't believe me, Whitney Sheppard, I'll just die!"

"And go to your tree?"

She was making fun of me, but I didn't blame her. Hearing myself say it made it sound loony toons even to me. Time for a do-over.

"Forget it. I just said that to make you feel better."

Whitney thought that through a moment, then rejected it.

"I think you meant it. But it still sounds a little…"

"Insane?" I prompted.

"Let's say hard to believe," then added, "When can we go?"

I couldn't believe my ears. "To the tree?"

"You said you've been there."

"I…well, I don't think non-Higglbys can even see it."

Whitney looked at the cherrywood box, then at me. She wiped away some tears. "Well, there's one way to find out."

I looked at her. "You believe me?"

"Let's just say I want to." She almost managed a smile.

We agreed to meet at the "No Trespassing" sign on Lime Street in the morning.

That night before I fell asleep, I cried for the first time—for the face, for the voice, for the space in rooms once filled by Grandmama Sheppard.

21
Tree for Two

As we trudged through the forest the next morning, I tried to explain Higglby Branchitivity to Whitney. I'm not sure she bought into it, but she was definitely intrigued.

When we passed the tree where Fief had gotten his head stuck, I got nervous. There was no Higglby tree. At least, not one I could see.

"Is it here?" Whitney asked, with a tinge of *what was I thinking* in her voice.

"I don't see it," I said. "But I told you, I'm not sure—"

Then it faded into view...the tree!

I held my breath. "Do you see it?"

"See what?"

"That tree there, with the trunk shaped like an H?"

"I just see regular old trees."

"Well, it isn't one. I've been inside it."

Whitney looked at me with sullen doubt creeping across her face.

"Wait here," I said.

Desperate to prove my point, I ran to the knothole to dive in. But instead of landing inside the tree, I was knocked backward onto the ground. I looked up and saw Fief. He had been coming out of the knothole just as I was going in.

"Sorry," he said, helping me up. "I heard your voice and was coming to tell you that Hugo wants to see you."

Then Fief saw Whitney. And from her shocked expression, I knew she saw him too.

"Who's this, then?" he asked. "Is she coming too?"

"I'm not sure she can. She's not a Higglby."

"Well, suit yourself, but let's go. It's my birthday, so after this, I'm taking the day off." With that, Fief plunged back into the tree.

I turned to Whitney. "Let me see what I can find out."

"Oh no, you don't!" Whitney scolded. "You aren't leaving me out here alone!"

"I have to. It's the only way!"

I put a hand on the tree to enter the knothole, but Whitney would have none of it. She grabbed my arm, then suddenly let go. Her eyes were big as saucers.

"I...I saw it."

"What?" I asked. It couldn't have been the tree. She didn't have any Higglby DNA, mutated or otherwise.

"When I touched you, I saw a tree."

Was it possible? I took her by the arm. "Do you see it now?"

She shook her head no. With my other hand, I touched the tree. A look of amazement flashed across her face.

"There it is!" she whispered. "D-d-does that mean *I'm* a Higglby?"

"I don't know what it means," I confessed. "But if you can see it when I'm touching both you and the tree, let's see if you can get in."

I grabbed her wrist and made my way through the knothole. Next thing I knew, we were both sprawled on the floor inside the tree. Whitney looked around.

"I don't believe it!" she gasped. "I'm in a tree!"

"You're in *the* tree," I bragged, "the Higglby Family Tree!"

There was nothing around us but the ladder until Fief poked his head through the mist in the ceiling. He smiled when he saw Whitney. "Another mutation, eh? Well, come along."

After I cleared the top of the ladder, Fief whispered, "She's a pretty one."

The three of us started down the hall until a long sword shot out in front of us. I heard Peerless's booming voice.

"Who goes there? Oh, it's you," he said when he saw Fief. "And that mutey-tated thing," he added when he saw me.

"We need the keys to 1785," Fief told him.

"This way," Peerless growled. Then he grabbed his back and yelled some things in—I'm guessing Nordic—that would've been bleeped on Viking television.

"Still got the back grabs, I see," Fief offered.

"Thanks to you and the devil," Peerless responded as we followed him into a gnarled cubicle. The room was full of odds and ends. But the main decor was a wall cluttered with keys.

"Who lives here?" I asked.

"No one lives here. It's my office," Peerless announced. Then he looked at Fief smugly. "An office means you're important."

Fief sniffed. "I'd rather have a tool belt. You can't make anything with an office."

"I can make a call and get you fired!" Peerless pointed to an old-fashioned phone hanging on the wall. "I have a tellyphone," he said proudly. "Something invented around branch 1900."

Then Peerless saw Whitney. "Another new Higglby? We're dropping like flies. Come here, you."

Whitney reluctantly stepped from behind Fief and me.

"Wait a minute, she don't look like no Higglby," Peerless growled. "She must've married in. I've got no clearance for her!"

"I can vouch for the lass. She's a Higglby," Fief lied.

"Maybe she is, and maybe she ain't. If she is, she'll be on the list. No one enters this tree without I check. What's your name?" Peerless demanded as he eyed Whitney warily.

"Whitney Sh—" Whitney caught herself before saying her real last name. "Shapelle...Whitney Shapelle Higglby."

"Hummph!" Peerless snorted. "Sounds French. I ain't fond of the French."

He toddled over to a wall and pulled down a chart with a jillion names scrawled on it.

"Well, is her name there?" Fief asked, unconcerned.

"Hard to say," Peerless muttered. "I can't read."

So that was why Fief wasn't worried. I pointed to the name Lucius Aloysius Higglby.

"There it is," I said. "Whitney Shapelle Higglby."

"All right, then," Peerless grumbled. "Carry on." He handed the key to Fief.

Whitney was gaining her courage. "I wasn't sure I'd be here after I died...I was cremated."

Peerless put both hands on his hips. "Why, that's a Viking funeral! The grandest there is!" He said it so proudly that Whitney couldn't help but smile.

Peerless shuffled some papers. "We'll have to be finding you a place to stay."

"Oh, I won't be staying," Whitney said.

Peerless froze in terror. "You better rethink that, missy. If anything happens to you whilst you're on the outside, your human form disappears forever. I lost my dearest comrade that way—and barely escaped with my own soul intact. I ain't been outside since."

Then he glared at me. "And you shouldn't be here at all, you alive little freak."

I saw the list the professor had given him still stuck in his belt. I got an idea.

"I came for that poultice list. No need of you risking your neck to save your back."

Peerless softened considerably. "Well, if that's your reason." He snatched the list from his belt and handed it to me. Then he eyed Whitney again with suspicion. "I'm wonderin' if maybe you ain't dead yourself. You who 'won't be staying.'"

Whitney took the high road and admitted it. "You're right; I'm still one of the undead."

Then, god love her, Whitney joined me back on the low road. "I just dropped by to give Fief a birthday present."

She pulled a container from her backpack with a chocolate frosted cupcake in it. Fief was elated. Peerless wasn't.

"Nothin' for me?" he pouted.

"Is it your birthday too?" Whitney asked.

"Since I don't know when my birthday is, then it just might be. I'll let it go this time, but from this day hence, stay out of the tree 'til you're here for the forever!"

As soon as we left the office, I heard Fief and Whitney giggle. I would've joined them, but I make it a point never to laugh at a man wearing a sword on one side and an ax on the other.

22
The Bundle

"Who's this Hugo guy?" Whitney whispered as we approached his door.

I told her about the box I found in the hidey-hole. "He probably just wants to thank me."

But the big husky man who opened the door had more to say than that. His eyes peered at me above a bushy gray beard.

"Well, you don't look French, and you don't look Sioux. But, *mon dieu*! You do look like a bowl full of Higglby!" he said with a wisp of a French accent.

He invited us into his rustic room, then fastened his gaze on me. "I am Hugo, your great-grandfather many times past."

"Hugo is the first Higglby born in America," Fief said proudly. "His people are from France."

"How did they get *here*?" Whitney asked.

"In a big hurry!" Hugo rasped. "We were Huguenots… Protestants in France, which was a *very* Catholic country. The king of France, he took away all our liberties but would not let us leave the country because of our skills and knowledge. We were forced to stay under penalty of death. But we left anyway—under penalty of 'catch us if you can!'" Hugo laughed.

"So you're Hugo the Huguenot," Whitney confirmed.

Hugo chuckled. "Yes, my little girl's little friend. You may not know, but our family is not so good with names."

"She's had a few clues," I said. "They named me Kitten."

"They named you a baby cat? Now *I* don't feel so bad. But be proud, little one. Many leaders in your war for independence were of Huguenot descent. Paul Revere—his father was a Huguenot. George Washington—grandson of a Huguenot! I, of course, was a farmer until my uncle convinced me to join him as a trapper on the Missouri River.

"So many of us left France, they finally quit pestering us. But too late! By then, France's vein was open, and her best blood had run to other soil—a half million of her best citizens."

"You were the first Higglbys on the Higglby farm?" I asked.

"*Oui!* Only it was the Higglbier farm—our French name. Then Higglberry. Then"—he made a chopping motion—"cut down to Higglby. Mon dieu!"

I had to ask. "What does 'mon dieu' mean?"

Hugo looked shocked. "You don't know what mon dieu means? Mon dieu!"

"It means 'my god,'" Whitney offered.

A girl, maybe five years older than me, entered the room.

Hugo smiled. "But enough about me. I want you to meet your grandmother many times past."

I waited for the girl to announce my distant grandmother's entrance, but first, she looked at Whitney and me. "Which of you is Kit?"

"I am," I said. I didn't understand her confusion. Whitney's brown skin and high cheekbones looked a little like this girl's, but I had all the other Higglby traits.

Then the girl said, "I am Sesapa, your grandmother many times past."

I stared. "But you aren't much older than I am!"

"I was eighteen when I died. But Hugo and I had already had two children together."

I gulped. "You're only eighteen, but you're my great-great... ever-so-great-grandmother?"

"We were both young then," Hugo added. "But after she died, I continued to age. Now I look like *her* grandfather, oui?"

Sesapa's dark brown eyes accented the thick black hair neatly braided over her shoulders. She wore a soft leathery dress with leggings and moccasins, all decorated with fringes and beads.

"You look like a Native American," I puzzled.

She smiled. "Did you not know you have Lakota blood?"

"I don't even know what Lakota is."

"It's a tribe of American Indians," Hugo informed me. "We French called them Sioux."

Sesapa scowled. "Some of us were not pleased with that name. It was a spiteful name given to us by an enemy tribe. It means 'little snakes.'"

Hugo sighed. "You live, you learn, you die, and they still never let you forget! But I thank you for returning my memoir box. You don't know how overjoyed she was to see it again."

That's when I noticed Sesapa clutching the leather pouch I'd found in the hidey-hole. She stared at it with reverence.

"This bundle is sacred to my tribe. We sometimes call it a medicine bag. I have been saddened by its loss for many years."

"Hugo knew where it was. Why didn't he come to the house to get it?" I asked.

"We cannot get very close to a place where we once existed," Hugo explained. "I've tried, but some kind of force keeps me away. And I didn't want Sesapa to break in. She might have been shot or arrested. Too dangerous!"

Sesapa stared at me like she was trying to see into my soul. Then she spoke. "You know what is in here?"

I shook my head. "The note said not to open it, so I didn't."

Hugo heaved another guffaw. "See, Sesapa? I told you no one could retie one of my knots without my knowing! I could tell she did not even try."

"It's a special knot?" Fief asked.

"A double constrictor," Hugo said proudly. "Most sailors cannot even tie it right."

"The important thing is I can trust you," Sesapa said to me. Then desperation clouded her face.

"I need your help. This bundle holds the most sacred objects of our tribe. They entrusted my father with its safety. But one day, our enemies were preparing to attack. He took one item from the bundle to wear into battle. Then he handed me the sacred pouch and sent me away to protect it."

"Why you?" Whitney asked.

"The tribal leaders believed my dreams were powerful, which meant I had the gift of the spirits. I was sent south with the bundle to stay with another Lakota tribe until it was safe to return. But the snows came. I was captured by an enemy tribe, then sold to Frenchmen for food and guns."

"I bought her to save her from those scoundrels," Hugo said. "We searched for her tribe but could not find them. So we went to live with the Brulé—a band of the Lakota."

Sesapa took his hand. "I died soon after giving birth to our second child."

Hugo saddened. "That is when I returned to the farm with our two children. I never remarried. But I put the sacred bundle in the safest place I knew and raised our *enfants* before I died of a broken heart."

Sesapa gave him a wry smile. "Broken heart—you died from being kicked by a horse."

"That's what broke it," Hugo said. "Also both my lungs."

"It's still sad," I said.

Hugo waved it off. "Eh, a horse kicks, you go 'oof,' you die and go to your tree. But the box stayed hidden all these years."

"Why do you need my help?" I asked Sesapa.

She grew solemn. "The first story I learned at my mother's knee was that of the white buffalo stone. It tells of a spiritual woman who presented our tribe with a bundle containing sacred items. Then, the woman walked from the tipi and lay down in the grass. When she rose, she had turned into a white buffalo calf.

"The Lakota follow the sacred rites she had taught them. But only *our* tribe had an actual white buffalo bestowed on it—a white stone shaped by the Creator into a white buffalo. It is our most sacred possession."

Sesapa touched the bundle hanging from her belt. "The sacred objects of the tribe are kept here, each wrapped carefully so they might never touch the ground. The only one missing is the white buffalo stone my father kept the day I was sent away."

Sesapa trembled now as she spoke. "Two sleeps ago, I had a dream that the white buffalo stone was about to be sold."

"Her dreams are powerful things," Hugo advised. "I learned to believe them."

I could feel how much the thought of the stone being sold hurt her. But even if it were true, I had no clue how I could help. Then Whitney spoke up.

"Kit's dad is an antique collector. He could do a data search."

I nodded toward Whitney. "That's why I brought her—she's smarter than I am. But even if we found it, how would we know it was the right one?"

"The stone was not carved by human hands. It was carved by the mountains," Sesapa explained. "That's why it is so remarkable. The stone is not only in the shape of a buffalo, it has an image of the Lakota medicine wheel on its back—not carved by man, but by nature."

I promised Sesapa I'd try to locate the stone.

After we left the tree, Whitney and I were quiet for a while.

Whitney finally spoke. "You found that pouch but didn't open it…you really are someone who can be trusted."

"I told *you* about the tree," I said, feeling I was on shaky ground.

Whitney smiled. "For all the right reasons. I won't betray your trust."

23
A Man, a Plan...

It's never a good thing to find myself starting a sentence with "Now, Dad, don't get mad…" But that was why Dad was giving me the stink eye. I think he knew what was coming next.

I told him I'd gone back to the tree. Then I told him one of his great-great-ever-so-great-grandmothers was a Lakota Indian. Then I hit him with the clincher.

"There's a sacred white buffalo rock that belongs to her tribe, but she thinks it's being sold somewhere. I told her you were good at finding old things."

I braced myself for the lecture. But Dad just took out his phone and went to work. Eventually, he hit pay dirt. "You're right. There's one being auctioned off in New York City."

A place called Master's Auctions had posted a pic of a white buffalo stone to be auctioned next week.

Dad googled further. "It's stirring up interest from protest groups."

One story quoted a protester: "Sacred items of the American Indian do not and should not have commercial value. These things were stolen from us."

Another article: "Tribal members say that outsiders who sell or even photograph sacred artifacts are committing a sacrilege—one more insult to the First People."

We looked at each other.

"It may not do any good, but are you up for a day trip to the Big Apple tomorrow?" Dad asked.

I was. I called Whitney to tell her what we'd found.

"You don't think they'll just hand it over, do you?" Whitney said in disbelief.

"No, but Dad's pretty good at bartering—I'm just not sure he has anything they'll want."

"Maybe we can find something," Whitney said with a hint of intrigue. "One thing we'll need is a poultice. The other thing is a cake."

While Whitney was gathering ingredients, I went by the saddlery store and bought the biggest air vest I could find, then got some heat packs from the pharmacy.

Whitney arrived at the farmhouse and whipped up a cake. The cake was from a mix, but the icing was a work of art.

That done, we went to work on the poultice. We heated a big pot of the ingredients on the professor's list: coconut oil, turmeric, ginger, onion, and garlic. When everything was steaming hot, we poured the stinky gruel into the vest. Then we stuffed the vest in the backpack and lined it with heat wraps to keep it warm.

When we got to the tree, Whitney grabbed my arm and we climbed through the knothole. Our first stop was Peerless's office. He jumped up to yell at me, but before he could, he grabbed his back and fell to the couch. I held up the vest.

"I brought your poultice as soon as I could."

The smell was almost unbearable to me, but Peerless sniffed the air with delight.

"My poultice! And I can wear it!"

I helped him put the vest on, and he sighed with relief—until he saw Whitney.

"You!" he growled. "If you ain't dead, you're about to be!"

A healthy Peerless might have followed through with his threat, but right now, Whitney knew she had the upper hand.

"I came to make a trade." She let that sit in the air a moment.

Peerless took the bait. "What kind of trade?"

Whitney placed her frosted gem in front of him. She had iced the cake in his likeness.

Peerless was awestruck. "It's like lookin' in a mirror!" Then, trying to control his eagerness, he added, "What's the trade?"

Whitney spotted a drinking horn hanging on the wall that must've come from a strange kind of cow. It also looked to be trimmed with brass.

"How about that drinking horn?" Whitney offered.

"Done! I picked that up in my plundering days, but I haven't used it since I found me this!" Peerless held up a stainless steel beer stein with "US Navy" emblazoned on it. "Even if I throw this at someone, it don't break!"

"Where'd you get that?" I asked.

"Funny thing that," Peerless mused. "Before I quit leaving the tree, I used to stretch my legs a bit outside the knothole.

One day, this old man sees me, so I ask if he has any mead on him. He says no, so I figure that's the end of it. But some weeks later, I find this here vessel outside sittin' atop a jug of mead! Every new moon for a couple of years, I'd find another jug. Then…nothin' 'til he showed up here in the tree one day. I haven't seen him since. Folks say he likes to keep to himself. But I still got me this drinky thing that don't break."

Whitney shouldered the drinking horn. "Aren't you going to eat your cake?"

"Not 'til I show it to that pinheaded Fief. He ain't never seen the likes of this!"

We left the tree with what we hoped would be a prized Viking drinking horn.

"You think that trim is real brass?" I asked.

Whitney smiled. "With any luck, it's gold."

I decided not to tell Dad about Whitney being in the tree, so just he and I trucked to New York City the next day. We arrived at the auction house at the appointed time but were told to wait.

I was admiring the felt-lined box Angie had put the drinking horn in when I remembered what Peerless had said.

"Dad, did you ever have a US Navy beer stein?"

"No, but Granddad did. Why?"

"Someone left one by the tree several years ago with a jug of mead."

"Who told you that?"

"The Viking this horn belonged to."

Dad began putting puzzle pieces together in his head. "Maybe that's why Granddad was making mead. He wasn't drinking it; he was taking it to the tree."

That's when the auction house manager invited us into her office.

"Sorry I'm late, but I got blindsided by some of those damnable protesters. You'd think they'd have better things to do," she muttered with a wee bit of contempt.

She and Dad exchanged some small talk then got down to business. The auction lady moved a glass display case toward us so we could see the stone inside.

The white buffalo was amazing! Dad and I both examined it. It did, indeed, have a small, almost imperceptible image of a medicine wheel on its back. And don't laugh, but it seemed to look lost, or lonely, or both—maybe because the case was so big and the stone was small. But I still couldn't shake the feeling.

The woman opened with "You're interested in this exquisite white buffalo stone?"

"Let's say I'm interested in returning it to its rightful owner," Dad countered.

The woman's face clouded. "You aren't here with those protesters, are you?"

"Just one," Dad said. "The woman whose family it was stolen from."

"And whose family is that?"

"Mine." Dad now showed a half smile. "But lawsuits are expensive and time-consuming. So I'm here to offer you a trade."

The woman matched his half smile. "It would have to be something pretty special. This is a spectacular rarity." The other half of her smile showed up.

Dad never flinched. "With all the laws against selling Native American pieces these days, I think you'll make a lot more money and have an easier time selling this…"

He laid our velvet box on her desk. She lifted the lid and saw the horn. Her smile twitched.

"A Norse drinking horn." She turned it over in her gloved hand and put on some special glasses. "The trimming is—"

"Solid gold," Dad finished for her.

"This looks like the horn of an aurochs," the woman mused.

"Which went extinct in seventeenth-century Europe," Dad added. "Do we have a deal?"

The woman took off the glasses and leaned back in her chair.

"Yes, Mr. Higglby, I believe we do."

24
Keys, Please

I could hardly wait to show Sesapa the stone, but Whitney had been the brains behind our success, so I waited for her to get off work from the bakery. We met at the tree.

Peerless was friendlier since the cake bribe, but he still demanded to know what business we had in the tree. We showed him the beautiful white buffalo stone and told him how important it was to Sesapa. Peerless rang up Fief on the "tellyphone," gave him the key, and soon we were back in Sesapa and Hugo's niche.

Her face lit up when she saw the stone.

"I dreamt you had found it!" she cried. "But I wouldn't let myself believe it until now." She pulled the pouch with the beadwork off her belt and left the room.

"It is a private thing to open the bundle," Hugo explained. "There are prayers to say."

Sesapa soon returned wearing the pouch and the biggest smile I've ever seen on such a small face.

"The bundle is whole once more. I owe you more than I can say in words."

Then she turned solemn again. She looked at Hugo, then at us. "The person chosen to carry the sacred bundle carried it for the people, not for themselves. My tribe entrusted me with their most treasured possession. I must return it to the land of my people."

"And where might that be?" asked Fief.

"A place called the Six Grandfathers in the Black Hills."

Hugo took both her hands in his big paws. "I will go with you."

Sesapa shook her head. "Your place is here."

"Well, you can't go alone," Whitney broke in.

"And you can't go to a place where people you know would be," Fief reminded her.

"It's a mountain," Sesapa explained. "I would only need to go far enough back in time that I can still find my way there."

Whitney thought. "The mid-1800s might work. The West still hadn't been settled yet."

"I'll talk to Peerless," Fief said, "but Whitney's right. You shouldn't go alone. I'll go with you, but I know nothing about the 1800s."

"I'd go," Whitney said, "but once I leave the tree, I can't get back in without Kit's help."

Suddenly, eight pairs of eyes were looking at *me*.

"You can't be serious," I finally sputtered. "I don't know anything about the Black Hills or the 1800s either."

Whitney was determined. "We'd know more than Sesapa does because we've studied history—well, one of us has. Besides, how many people get to *see* history? It's a no-brainer!"

That was precisely the amount of brains I'd need to agree, I thought, but all those eyes were still staring. I'd spent most of my life being ashamed of my ancestors. It never occurred to me they might be the ones ashamed of me.

"Well...if you can get the keys from Peerless."

Fief heaved a worried sigh. "He's not the most cooperatin' fellow--especially with tree keys. He takes his job very seriously."

It was time to jump in with both feet. I turned to Whitney. "You know that mead your dad's been making? Peerless loves it!"

Whitney got a sparkle in her eye. "Be right back."

Fief went with Whitney to escort her down to the knothole. While we waited, I noticed a sharp pointy thing on the floor and picked it up.

"That's a porcupine quill," Sesapa said. "I use it in my sewing." She showed me the design on her medicine bundle made with dozens of quills.

"How can you collect so many?"

"If we women found a porcupine, we would throw a blanket over it. The porcupine would raise his quills, and they'd get caught in the blanket."

She took a small doll from a bag she was packing. "This is a bead-and-buckskin doll."

The doll was truly a work of art. Sesapa explained that its hair was made from buffalo-calf hair. Quills were used as decorative staples. The doll's dress even had a little medicine bag hanging from its waist.

"These dolls were a treasured gift from a grandmother. Mine made this one to look like me. I have kept it with me always."

Fief returned from the tree trunk to report that Whitney was back, so I went to give her my "helping hand" through the knothole. To my surprise, she returned with the mead and her backpack bulging with who knows what. I thumped it like a watermelon.

Whitney shrugged. "Just some things we might need for the trip. I even brought you a sunbonnet."

"I don't wear sunbonnets," I scoffed.

"Then I will," she announced and put it on.

"We can't go *now!*" I yelled.

"Why not? Time stands still here. We'll be back before anyone knows we're gone."

"Wait a minute!" I demanded. "We have to think this through. We'll be going back to a time when women didn't have any rights. And neither did kids—especially girl kids! We won't be able to go anywhere we want, or do anything we want, or even say anything we want."

"The women who had courage enough to live through that are the reason we're here," Whitney said. "Should they expect less from *us?*"

Wow! She was good. She knew she had me, so she turned to Fief. "But it would help if we had someone older and stronger with us too."

If Fief were a balloon, he would've burst. The kid is *not* good at flirting. He started nodding like a bobblehead.

Sesapa joined us in Peerless's office, but Peerless, as predicted, was in no mood to hand over the key—until Whitney held up the jug of mead. Peerless looked at the jug like I'd look at a prancing pony.

"Here's what I'll do," he offered. "I won't give you the key, but I'll go with you and open the door."

Whitney handed him the jug. Then, to everyone's amazement, he suddenly handed it back. "I can't let the whole lot of you go. It's too dangerous."

"I must go," Sesapa said. "Even if I go alone. It has weighed on my soul too long."

"And I'm going with her," I chimed in. Then I remembered the motto I'd written on my dry-erase board. "It's like Wayne Gretzky said, 'you miss one hundred percent of the shots you never take!'"

"Who's Wayne Gretzky?" Fief asked.

"What's a shot?" Peerless added.

Whitney took over. "Come on, Peerless, you're a Viking! You're loud and you're proud!"

Peerless paused, then threw back his shoulders and grabbed the key. With that, we were off on the first leg of our journey—a trip through the tree!

Peerless took the lead. He quickly found the offshoot branch that would lead us west. Then we started a search for the branches that would take us back to the proper time.

"Which year should we look for?" Fief asked.

"After the Civil War would be safest, so around 1865," Whitney suggested.

It was during this part of the search that the branches became hopelessly tangled.

"Ain't it your job as tree carpenter to fix this?" Peerless asked as we stumbled to a halt.

"Do you know how many limbs are on just one branch, you big baboon?" Fief shot back.

"I only need one to throw you from," Peerless grumbled.

Fief took another step, then fell through some branches and disappeared. We heard a thud.

"Everything all right down there?" Peerless yelled.

No answer.

Peerless turned to me. "Go check on him—unless you're one of the cowardly Higglbys."

"I'm not a coward."

"Good! 'Cause there's too many of us as it is."

That's when Fief yelled up, "I've found a way out!"

We climbed down and found ourselves in a small cubicle with a knothole. Sesapa brushed away some branches, and light poured in. But when we started to exit, Peerless held back.

"Come on, Peer," Fief exhorted. "Where's your itch for adventure?"

"Last time I scratched it, my best friend got disappeared—just like the professor warned."

"What happened?" I asked.

"Thornjab got bored hanging around the tree, so we decided to ransack—I mean, visit the New World. But before you could say, 'skoldefroon,' we're in a fight with pirates. Thorny got himself run through with a sword."

Peerless's head sagged to his chest. "He ain't been seen since—gone forever!"

He gave Sesapa a warning look. "It taught *me* the danger of leaving this tree."

"I know the danger," Sesapa admitted. "But I still must go."

"Me too," Fief said with determination. "It's not just a mission—it's a Higglby mission."

"That's true," I added proudly. "What we need is a Higglby cheer."

"I'm not a Higglby," Whitney whispered in my ear.

"This trip makes you an honorary one—but I wouldn't put it on your résumé," I whispered back.

"I remember one," Peerless announced and shouted:

"Higglbys forever! God save the clan!"

"I'm not yelling that," Whitney muttered in my ear.

"How about our own special one," I suggested. "Like…"

Whitney jumped in with:

*"Higglbys will always roam!
Let's go find Sesapa's home!"*

"Honorary Higglbys don't get to make up cheers," I muttered. "But that's pretty good."

We all did the cheer and ended with a rousing fist bump and a *"Go-o-o-o, Higglbys!"*

But as we crawled out of the knothole, Peerless stayed back.

"May Thor give you wings!" he yelled as we left the tree. To me, he added, "I've got me this tree map to study. It's like a chart of the ocean, but with branches instead of currents and such."

I nodded, gave him another fist bump, then climbed out of the knothole into the Wild West!

25
Brave Old World

What we saw around us in this new world was more woods. We could've been back in the Forbidden Forest for all I knew. We walked a few minutes, then emerged from the trees and saw we were on a hillside.

There was a town off in the distance. Then a wagon came rattling down a road below us. Sesapa ducked out of sight. But when the woman in the wagon saw the rest of us, she had the man pull the horses to a halt.

"Well, would you look at that? Where in the world are *you* kids from?" she yelled.

"We're...waiting for our folks," I answered.

The woman gasped. "She's a young lady! Does your mother let you dress like that, child?"

Uh-oh. Whitney's and my jeans were clearly not in fashion around here.

Whitney pulled her sunbonnet lower over her face and yelled down, "We're from the hill country. All we have are these britches."

"Britches?" I muttered under my breath.

"Huckleberry Finn—read a book!" Whitney muttered back.

"Our parents went to town to buy us some clothes," Fief added.

"The wagon train's pullin' out tomorrow—last one this year. Your folks best get a move on if they're leavin' with it," the man said.

Fief nodded. "I'll tell 'em, mister. What's that town's name again?"

"Independence! Don't you kids know nothin'?" the woman harped.

The man pulled what looked like a flyer from his coat pocket. "Your folks can have this if they've a need."

Fief scrambled down the hill and took it. As the wagon moved on, we huddled around the flyer. It read, "Supplies needed for Oregon Trail." Beneath it was a list of items and how much they cost. But what caught my eye was the date: Spring 1855.

Whitney was still examining her clothes. "I don't know about Sesapa's outfit, but you and I stand out like two radishes in an order of fries."

"We need a plan," I said.

"I thought this *was* our plan," Fief retorted.

"A better one!" I frowned.

We headed back to the tree and huddled in the trunk again. I took charge. "Okay, we need clothes, transportation, and money to buy both." I dug into my pocket and came up with two twenties. "I have forty dollars."

"If you try to spend that, they'll either arrest you for counterfeit or hang you as a witch," Whitney said.

"Oh, right," I realized. "We need *their* money—whatever that is."

"And what about Sesapa?" Whitney asked. "I wonder what the laws are about Indians around here."

I looked at Whitney. "What about you?"

"What about me?" Whitney said. "You nimrods freed us, remember?"

I pointed to the date on the flyer—1855. "Isn't that *before* the Civil War?"

Whitney drew back. "Oh crap!"

I looked at the new Rolex watch Mom had given me. I took it off and handed it to Fief.

"Okay, new plan! Take this into town. It's real gold, so don't let them lowball you. If anyone asks, just say you traded some horses for it. Get as much as you can, then find a store that sells clothes and buy three dresses cheap."

Fief gulped. "You want *me* to buy dresses?"

"Yes—because your mama sprained her ankle."

"Can I buy a hat for me?" he asked.

"Sure."

"And one for Kit," Whitney added and gave me a look. "Trust me, you're going to need one."

Deciding a new hat was a fair trade for his embarrassment, Fief nodded and popped back out of the tree.

Peerless peered down at us from above.

"What's all the fuss and feathers about?" He lowered himself into the cubicle. "Back already?"

"We went a few years too far back," Whitney explained. "But those branches are so tangled, we might be better off not looking for another year."

She took a map out of her bulging backpack. "Still think it's overstuffed?" she asked me.

She'd definitely thought further ahead than the rest of us She spread the map out and explained.

"The Black Hills are up here in South Dakota. It's Indian land. Even today, most of it is a national park. It's unlikely a Higglby ever died there—so no knothole. We're down here near Independence, Missouri—the start of the Oregon Trail. If we can find an exit in the tree farther west into Nebraska territory, I think I'll be fine. Nebraska wasn't even a state back then so no slave laws."

"I was studying my tree map while waitin' for you fine folks to get yourself killed," Peerless interjected. "There's an offshoot branch a bit farther that might work."

We decided it was worth a try, so we waited for Fief to return.

"What do Higglbys do here in the tree to pass the time?" I asked Peerless.

"Some are like Fief is—and like I used to be," Peerless said. "They go explorin' because they miss the sounds and smells of the World. But that's dangerous, so most prefer to stay in their branch and talk about old times. They give themselves the gift of contentment."

"I will have contentment someday—when my spiritual obligation is finally fulfilled," Sesapa said meekly, then looked at us. "I realize now I could not have done this alone."

Eventually, Fief returned wearing a western hat and carrying a satchel full of dresses and aprons—and a bonnet for lucky me.

Whitney took a pink dress. Sesapa chose the yellow one, and I got stuck with a dull gray one. But the bag still wasn't empty. I pulled out a pair of white frilly leggings.

"They're pantaloons," Fief said, turning cherry red. "The shopkeeper said no respectable female would be without 'em. And I don't care to be hanging around with no other kind, thank you very much."

"Do you have any money left?" I asked hopefully.

Fief grinned. "Almost twenty-five dollars!" He handed me a bag of silver dollars.

I don't think the exchange rate would thrill Mom, but it is what it is, I thought as Peerless guided us to a different branch.

The branches were like a toll road, only you had to pay with cuts and scratches to get through.

After a slight search, Fief announced he'd found a way out and left the tree to do more reconnaissance work since he was the most inconspicuous of our group. When he returned, he announced we were in Nebraska near Fort Kearny—the last supply stop on the Oregon Trail.

"They said it's a fort, but it looks like a regular town. There isn't even a wall around it."

"How are they dressed?" I asked.

"The Indian women dress like Sesapa—but you and Whitney will need those dresses. And we'll need to buy a wagon and horses."

"Or find a ride with someone who already has them," I suggested. "Either way, we're going to need more money."

"If this is the last supply stop for wagon trains, there might be a need for hired help," Whitney said.

"Get a job?" I whined. Whitney glared at me.

"I don't mind working," I snapped. "I just don't know anything I'm good at."

She smiled menacingly. "We'll find you something."

With that, Whitney and I changed into proper young-lady attire, hoping to find proper young-lady work.

Then, once again, we said goodbye to Peerless and left the tree.

26
Wagon Ho!

Fief was right. Fort Kearny looked nothing like a military fort and everything like an 1850s strip mall. Anything that could be sewn, grown, or slaughtered was for sale.

There were almost as many Indians selling their wares as there were soldiers and people from wagon trains. Girls my age were in ankle-length dresses with long sleeves. I caught a glimpse of myself in a bug-splattered mirror hanging just inside a covered wagon. All things considered, I looked pretty darn stylish.

We split up to look for work, so I wandered around. I saw some musicians playing at the end of the street. It was nothing I would dance to, but without Valerie and Crystal around to hog the spotlight, I might be able to snag some attention. I tied my bonnet under my chin with a jaunty bow and started toward the festivities.

Suddenly, I was blindsided by a blast of prairie wind. It blew the bonnet off my head and wrapped my dress around me like I was a tetherball pole. After chasing down my hat, I decided it was time to get a job.

Ficf found work wrangling livestock. I knew horses better than he did. I'd even mucked out stalls. But in 1855, those jobs were for men only. I was beginning to see why Susan B. Anthony always looked mad enough to spit nails.

I passed a store called the Mercantile selling stuff like darning wool. Since I didn't know what a mercantile or darning wool was, I didn't think that would be a good fit. Instead, I got work in a kitchen—also not a good fit. But I learned why womenfolk wear aprons. It's the best way to carry bulky items—except eggs.

Sesapa was mending clothes. But it was Whitney who hit the jackpot. People paid her to sketch their pictures and paint mottoes on the canvas of their wagons. Slogans like "Oregon or Bust" and "Lord Bless This Wagon" began to liven up the scenery.

When demand tapered off, Whitney, Sesapa, and I went wagon to wagon offering to load stuff like bales of hay. During this venture, I saw a man arriving at the fort—an odd-looking fellow with a big diamond-shaped head. He had a full wagon that needed unloading, and that was proving to be my best, possibly only, useful skill.

"Need some help?" I asked, running over. "It'll only cost you a quarter."

"Unload 'em over there by the mercantile and I'll give you a dime," he said like he'd said it a hundred times before. He pulled back a canvas tarp to reveal a wagonload of big pots.

"What are these for?" I asked, thinking maybe I should take them to the kitchen.

"They're piss pots, of course. Grown-ups use 'em, then you kids empty 'em out."

"Why us kids?" I asked, turning up my nose.

"'Cause that's what kids are for," he said. "Now get to it."

As I unloaded the pots, he unhitched his horses. I could tell he was especially fond of one of the lead horses. I heard him call her Sassy.

"You want me to take her to the stable for you?"

"Nah, thanks. She's used to me. We've been together a long time, Sassy and me."

I immediately liked the guy—not enough to empty his piss pot, but enough to ask him where he was headed.

"West to Scottsbluff, then north a piece. Gonna trade for pelts up in the Black Hills."

When I heard "Black Hills," I started unloading pots so fast anyone watching must have thought I needed one. I finished the job and found him in the stable.

"Your pots are unloaded," I announced. Then added, "My name is Kit."

"Well, good," he said, then finally added, "They call me On-Time Taterhead."

"Why?" I had to ask.

"Because I used to haul spuds from the farms to the forts. And guess what?"

"You were always on time?"

Taterhead laughed and wiped his sweaty bald head—but he still only gave me a dime. I chatted with him some more, which turned out to be our lucky break.

I hurried to the spot Sesapa had picked out behind a store where our little group was planning to spend the night.

"We have a ride!" I announced. "His name is On-Time Taterhead, and—"

"Say that again?" Whitney broke in.

"I'm just the messenger," I said. "He's going to a trapper's camp near the Black Hills. We leave tomorrow at dawn."

"I'm ready now," Sesapa said.

"Do we have enough money?" Whitney asked.

I grinned. "More than enough. He's hiring Sesapa as a guide. He doesn't usually trade that far north, so I told him Sesapa knows that territory like the back of her hand."

"I hope so," Fief warned, "or he's likely to give us the back of his."

Sesapa clutched the sacred bundle tied safely around her dress. "I will get us there."

On-Time Taterhead wanted to get out in front of the wagon train because of the dust. There would be lots of dust—from the wind, from other wagons, and churned up by livestock the emigrants were moving along the trail with them. So before the sun was up, we were.

Taterhead's wagon was half empty on this leg of the trip, so we'd be making good time. While we hitched up his wagon, he squinted a serious look at Sesapa.

"You sure you know the lay of the land up near the Black Hills, little lady?"

"Yes. My name Sesapa means Black Hills."

"I'm lookin' for a place the Indians call zaka laka."

Sesapa smiled. "I think you mean xoká ohlóka. It's Lakota for Badger Hole."

"Then Zoka loka Badger Hole it is!" Taterhead announced. Then he turned his stare on the rest of us.

"Now, what exactly are four young'uns doin' out here by themselves?" He looked to Fief for an answer. Fief was well rehearsed.

"Our daddy's a trapper. He sent us money to join him, but it ran out."

Taterhead looked us over. "You all had the same daddy, did ya?"

"He remarried an Indian woman," I said, weaving another lie into our tangled web.

He studied Whitney. "You might be part Indian—or you might be a runaway slave."

We froze. But before any of us could answer, Taterhead went back to loading the wagon.

"I got no quarrel with that. I don't hold with no man ownin' another. If a man's got work to do, he should do it his own self. Not glomming onto somebody else. A man's got to kill his own snakes."

"My dad says that!" I blurted out.

"Your daddy's right…too bad he's too cheap to come get you himself."

We breathed a collective sigh of relief. But the tater man turned and stared us down again.

"This here Oregon Trail is like wrestlin' a wild boar. It can eat you alive or you can eat it. Either way, you know you've been in a fight. Out there, the heat can scorch your brains. And it's drier than a dust devil—until it rains. Then folks get struck by lightning and killed by hail. You'll get wetter than a baby's butt and caked in mud enough to take a beaver to a barn dance.

You'll be workin' like a mule and eating like a horse, possibly with a horse—but only in an emergency. Now, are you little ankle-biters still interested?"

Fief put his hands on his hips. "Where do you want us to sit?"

Taterhead almost smiled.

We climbed in the wagon and were rolling out of the fort when we heard—

"Stop!"

We turned to see a small skinny man in a wilted suit running toward us. He reminded me of a chameleon the way he blended into the wagons and dust. He clutched an old banjo in one hand and a bulky canvas bag in the other that rattled as he slithered toward us.

"Have you got room for one more, my good fellow?" His voice seemed to drone on even after he stopped talking.

"We're leaving the trail after Scottsbluff," Taterhead told him.

"That'll do. The name's Slimrod Rumpwrath." He shook Taterhead's hand.

"I don't know…I've got these young'uns here. They—"

"Fifty dollars in gold?" the man offered, jingling a bag of coins.

Taterhead's eyes lit up like glow sticks. He took the bag of money. "Welcome aboard!"

So while this sleazy-looking dude sat in front with Taterhead, the four of us rode in the wagon bed. I amused myself by watching the wagon train take shape behind us. I could see why the wagons were called prairie schooners. A schooner is a sailboat, and the canvas bonnets over the wagons did look like sails from a distance. Our wagon didn't have a bonnet, just a canvas tarp to cover the supplies.

Then I noticed the rest of the scenery. It was amazing. This was tallgrass prairie country, and it was mesmerizing to watch grass taller than the horses swaying in the lazy breeze. I watched the white throats of antelope bounce through their playground while mega sunflowers waved from a distance.

But after several hours of bumping up and down like a jack-in-the-box, I got bored. I looked around to see what was sharing the wagon with us.

"What kind of stuff do you trade to the Indians?" I asked Taterhead.

"Oh, pots, mirrors, jackets, knives—lots of knives."

"Why so many knives?"

"Cause a knife's the most useful thing there is. They use 'em to put up tipis and mend moccasins, make clothing, make arrows, skin animals—"

"Okay, I get it," I said.

"Clean fish, build traps, scrape hides, take scalps—"

"All right! I give up!" I pleaded. Then I spotted Slimrod Rumpwrath's bag.

27
The Awakening

Slimrod was sound asleep in the buckboard seat, so I sneaked a peek in his bag. It was full of bottles labeled "Dr. Slim's Kickapoo Juice."

"He's a snake oil salesman," Whitney whispered. She explained that stuff like this used to be sold as medicine, but it usually contained alcohol, cocaine—even opium.

I found a tin box in the bag. What was in it looked and smelled like charcoal mixed with axle grease.

I didn't know what it was for, so I put it back and closed the bag. And not a minute too soon. Just then, Taterhead broke into one of his made-up songs and sang loud enough to wake the dead and Slimrod—or Slimewad, as I was beginning to think of him.

This song was to the tune of "Turkey in the Straw."

*"Well, I ain't got a dollar, and I ain't got a dime,
And I ain't got a blanket in the wintertime;
But I got me ol' Sassy, who's a-pulling at the wheel
And there ain't nobody who can best me in a deal."*

After a few verses, Taterhead had us get out of the wagon to look for buffalo chips—a polite term for buffalo poop. People on the prairie used it for firewood because there weren't many trees—but there sure must have been a lot of buffalo. When their poop dried, it turned into discs as hard as Frisbees. Sesapa was familiar with the chips.

"In many ways, they are better than wood," she said. "They don't smell when they burn, and they make very little smoke."

Whitney and I worked as a team. She collected poop while I held my apron out like a basket.

"I hope we didn't make a big mistake coming out here," she confided in me. "When I volunteered us, I didn't know we'd have to get to the Black Hills by way of the Oregon Trail."

"So far, so good," I chirped, trying to sound upbeat.

"It's the 'so far' part that worries me." Whitney frowned. "At the fort, people were talking about how dangerous river crossings are. The worst one is only a few days from here."

"Can't you swim?"

"Sure, in a pool. But a river current is like an underwater hurricane."

I told her Taterhead knew what he was doing, and I believed that. Of course, I also believed Whitney wouldn't make *me* pick up the buffalo poop. I was naive.

Around sundown, we made camp and waited for the wagon train to catch up with us.

"No need spending nights out here alone," Taterhead noted. "Fewer people are going west this year because of the Indian wars. But most of that trouble's up around Oregon."

"The Indians didn't start it," Sesapa responded. "They are only fighting back like you would against a horde of locusts."

"You got that right," Taterhead said. "So many of them gold diggers came through here on their way to Californee they used up all the oxen—the emigrants are down to horses and mules."

I helped Fief unhitch our four horses, glad *they* weren't oxen. The lead horse was Sassy, and her harness mate was Buster. Chick and Charlie were the wheelers—the horses closest to the wagon. They just followed along, doing only what they had to…kind of like me.

We were waiting for the wagon train to find us, but the mosquitoes found us first.

"Got any bug repellent in that backpack?" I asked Whitney.

"No, but Huck Finn smeared onion tops on his skin to get rid of them."

"There you go with Huckleberry Finn again. Wasn't that book banned?"

"The original one was—mostly by white people in the South. And not because of the n-word. They didn't like being portrayed as hicks. They also said it didn't agree with their values."

"Why?"

Whitney gave me that slow head turn.

"Okay, so I haven't read it."

Whitney sighed. "Mark Twain was one of the first American writers to expose the lie that plantation life was a romantic existence full of happy, carefree slaves. The reader is forced to confront the depraved reality of enslavement."

"What happened in the story?"

"Huck helps free Jim. So basically, it's about an uneducated white boy who went against everything he'd been taught because his gut told him it was the right thing to do. Also, Jim was essentially the hero of the story—a Black hero in fiction was very rare back then."

Just then, a mosquito bit off a chunk of my cheek. I slapped it hard enough to knock a younger me unconscious.

"The Lakota painted their faces to keep mosquitoes away," Sesapa suggested.

"I thought that was war paint."

"Sometimes it was—but sometimes the war was against mosquitoes."

The wagon train arrived and began circling the wagons.

"Are they expecting trouble?" Fief asked Taterhead.

"Nah, they're forming a corral to keep the horses in."

Our little band sat down to bacon, bread, and beans cooked over a near-smokeless fire of buffalo chips. Unfortunately, the chips burn faster than wood. It took four or five apronfuls to cook dinner. I should have bought a bigger apron.

Slimewad didn't do any heavy lifting but ate plenty. When he finished, he announced he would be joining the emigrants for the evening.

"I always enjoy the stories and merriment present in large gatherings," he said with the pomposity of a lousy actor. "So I shall take my leave of you—'Sleep! O gentle sleep! Thou no more wilt steep my senses in forgetfulness.'"

I think he was fracturing Shakespeare, but whatever it was, he left to no applause. He took his banjo and canvas bag and slinked into the darkness. I just didn't like the man—his sweaty lip, his glossy eyes, or his smell of rancid grease.

After dinner, I stared at the fire's glow and breathed in the scent of leather, horses, and tallgrass in the evening air.

Before settling in for the night, I went to the wagon to get my backpack-slash-pillow. I could make out Taterhead's silhouette rummaging through the wagon.

"I've got an extra bedroll here somewhere if anybody needs a pillow," he said.

"Whitney and I are using our backpacks, but Sesapa might like one."

Taterhead took the bedroll to Sesapa. He squinted at her medicine bundle in the dim light. "You even sleep with that little bag on? Must be something mighty valuable in it," he teased.

"Only to me," she said and closed her eyes.

The night was calm, the stars were out, and I could hear the wagoners murmuring in the nearby camp. Then banjo music began to fill the air. Whitney and I decided to sneak over and check out the wagon train show. Sure enough, Slimewad was the star performer. He was singing, and telling jokes, and strumming his banjo. Then my jaw dropped. He was doing it in blackface!

Now I knew what was in the tin I'd found earlier. It was greasepaint. Slimrod was singing in a Southern accent and telling corny jokes in what I took to be slave lingo.

Whitney was furious, but before she could vault over one of the wagon tongues, I grabbed her. "We haven't had the Civil War yet. Don't push it."

"I've never felt freer or madder than right now," Whitney seethed.

Slimrod had stopped playing and was hyping his fake medicine when he saw Whitney coming toward him. The emigrants saw her too.

"Who are you to make fun of people forced to work for no wages? People who were stolen from their homes, stacked up like cordwood, and shipped across an ocean to be humiliated, and horsewhipped, and raped. Anyone who sees humor in that shouldn't be numbered as part of the human race!" Then she turned to the crowd.

"You people just left behind family and friends you may never see again. Well, so did they! Not because they were looking for a better life—but because they were kidnapped and sold into a worse one! Do you really find that funny?"

The wagon families, even those who were laughing earlier, went silent. Whitney stilled herself with a deep breath, then turned and left.

I followed her back to camp. I was now feeling both her anger and my shame for not having shared her rage before. Sesapa had heard Whitney, too, and took her hand.

"You were right to speak to them that way."

"They don't care," Whitney said, holding back tears. "They think I'm just a stupid kid."

"I don't," I said. "But *I've* sure been one. I should have been standing there beside you. Next time I will be."

Sesapa took my hand too. "There is a Lakota saying: 'A nation is not conquered until the hearts of its women are on the ground. Only then is it finished, no matter how brave its warriors or how strong their weapons.' That's why we must follow our heart when it demands our lips to speak."

Whitney smiled. "That sounds like something Grandmama Sheppard would say."

"Grandmothers can be very wise," Sesapa answered.

I now remembered this young girl *was* a grandmother—one of mine.

I smiled proudly. "Maybe that's why we call them grand."

28

Baubles, Bangles, and Burglary

The stars that night were more brilliant than I thought possible. My brain was filled with more light, too, as I began to see the world through other people's eyes. I looked over at Whitney.

"You awake?" She nodded.

"Got any star stories?"

She pointed out a bright star and said it belonged to the constellation Cygnus, the swan. "Zeus turned himself into a swan so he could swim through the Milky Way to have a love affair with some goddess."

Sesapa was awake too. She pointed to a group of stars near Cygnus. "To my people, those stars there are a turtle we call Keya. Like the Lakota, it carries its home on its back. It represents wisdom and perseverance."

I kind of liked that. It was better than picturing an old man skinny-dipping his way to a hot date.

Whitney turned to Sesapa. "I wish I understood your sacred bundle better. Why are the things in it so sacred?"

"To us, our bundle is sort of like your Bible."

"How? You can't read it."

"Each bundle contains objects of spiritual significance—a bird's feather, a lock of hair from a special horse, maybe a rock or a crystal. Things with meaning we meditate on."

"Oh, like Grandmama would sometimes read passages in the Bible that were important to her—those verses would be like items in your bundle."

Sesapa nodded. "That's why we sometimes call it our medicine bag. Most Lakota have a personal bundle. But the tribal bundle is the most holy of holies because it is believed beneficial to the entire tribe. It is opened only on special occasions in a precise ritual. And those items are meant to be kept secret by the keeper. They have been passed down from one keeper to another over such a long time their origins are shrouded in mystery."

Her deep sigh filled the quietness of the night.

"My soul has had little peace knowing our tribal bundle was entrusted to me only to be lost to its people for so long."

"We'll get it there," Whitney said with resolve.

Then, we thought our private thoughts as songs of the crickets and the howl of coyotes reclaimed the darkness.

The next morning we woke to the sound of On-Time Taterhead crowing like a rooster.

"Time for breakfast! You can have beans and bacon or bacon and beans."

I was hungry enough to eat buffalo chips but went with bacon and beans.

"I don't know how you do this every day of your life," I told Taterhead as we packed up the wagon.

"Wouldn't have it any other way," he said. "Travelin' is like writin' a song. Every day is a brand new tune."

Slimewad, unfortunately, had returned during the night and seemed as eager as Taterhead to get on the trail. He even helped hitch up the horses. The clod didn't speak to Whitney, but he didn't seem to care that she had crashed his party. He just coiled up on the buckboard seat and waited for us to get started. But Taterhead was having none of it.

"You ain't been pullin' your weight around here, Rumpwrath. Either help me grease this wheel or take your turn pickin' up buffalo chips today."

Slimy looked disgusted but went to the wheel. Taterhead handed him a bucket that had been hanging from the rear axle.

"What is that?" I asked Fief.

"It's grease made with animal fat and tar. You want some?"

"Maybe after we run out of bacon and beans."

I climbed in the wagon and sat down hard before realizing I had sat on Slimewad's bag. Afraid I had broken a bottle, I opened the bag expecting to see broken glass. What I saw was a bag full of jewelry—watches, necklaces...even gold coins!

Fief heard me gasp and leaned over to look.

"What's all this?" He pawed through the loot. "These things must belong to the people on the wagon train!"

We turned as one to look at Slimrod. He had heard Fief too.

"Get away from that, you ninnies, that's mine."

He sprinted over and snatched the bag. But Taterhead grabbed it and looked inside.

"You slimy buzzard! Why, you're nothin' but a cussid thief," Taterhead snarled. Then he saw the pouch of gold coins Slimrod had paid him also stuffed in the satchel.

"Why, you're lower than a bottomless well!" Taterhead seethed. "Them's the coins you paid me. You probably stole 'em back at Fort Kearny. Now you're stealing 'em back from me!"

Outnumbered, Slimewad turned into a whimpering mass of jelly. "I'm just trying to get by," he sniveled.

"Well, you ain't gettin' by!" Taterhead said through clenched teeth.

We followed Taterhead and the satchel as he marched to the wagon train where the emigrants were packing to move out. They weren't happy to hear they'd been robbed by the singing snake oil salesman.

"I'll shoot that scum!" one of them yelled. A group of men ran to Taterhead's wagon. The wagon was still there, but the Slimer was nowhere to be found. We combed the tallgrass and looked behind every rock. There was no sign of the thief.

29
The River

The wagon master finally called a halt to the search. Everyone had their valuables back, and they still had a schedule to keep.

We got on the trail ahead of the wagon train, and soon, hills began to break up the flat prairie. At one of the steeper climbs, we got out and walked beside the wagon to make it easier on the horses. That's when the topic of Slimewad came up again.

"I can't believe he stole back the money he paid Taterhead," Whitney said. "I'm surprised he didn't try to steal the buffalo stone in Sesapa's bundle too."

"He probably would've if he'd known how much it was worth," I said. "Dad thinks it would have gone for at least fifty thousand dollars in New York."

Possibly because of his tendency to get lost, Fief had become enthralled with a compass Whitney had brought along. She had shown him how to take bearings on a map, so now he was constantly tracking our progress. When we stopped to rest the horses, Fief took a map out to study it.

"So where are we?" I asked. "And I want names, not latitudes and longitudes."

"Scottsbluff is here in the Nebraska panhandle," Fief reported. "That's where we'll turn north and end up here in South Dakota."

"We should charge you tutoring fees," Whitney announced.

"Not interested. But if there's a motor scooter in that backpack, I'll pay you plenty."

"No sale," Whitney chuckled. "You're finally getting a few muscles in those toothpick legs of yours."

We were trekking through "the wilderness," but reminders of the thousands of people who traveled this route were ever present. Many parts of the trail had become junk heaps as possessions in overloaded wagons were shed along the way. Broken wagon parts, empty food barrels, furniture, clothes, books—even a piano sat rotting in the sun.

Sometimes Taterhead stopped to sift through the once treasured belongings. It reminded me of trips I'd made with Dad. At one spot, Taterhead picked up some flannel shirts and a comb.

I shook my head. "Finding stuff to trade is hard work."

Taterhead shook *his* head. "Trading is like playing a guitar; you just have to know which notes to pick." Then he leaned in and asked, "Does your little friend have anything in that pouch she might be willing to deal for?"

"No, it's a Lakota thing. Just good luck charms—but religious."

We soon came across the grandest thing I've ever seen—a prairie-dog town! As far as I could see were thousands of black-tailed prairie dogs sitting beside a thousand holes. I loved watching them hold their paws up like they were praying. If they were, it was probably for all these wagons to go away.

Suddenly, the prairie dogs disappeared so fast I thought I'd imagined them. Then all hail broke loose—and I mean hail! The sky opened up like it was having a nervous breakdown. First rain—then hailstones. Huge hailstones!

I'd noticed a little black cloud earlier, but Mother Nature had my full attention now as lightning strikes began flying out of huge black clouds circling above us.

Zeus isn't messing around, I thought. The loudest thunder crashes ever banged at our ears while the wind whipped sheets of rain at our throats.

Taterhead had warned us that these prairie hailstorms could be lethal. Now I believed him. It was the worst game of dodgeball ever! It pelted us with an assist from the roaring wind, which almost knocked the wagon off the road.

Fearful of a lightning strike, Taterhead ordered us to unhitch the horses. We freed them from the harness shaft. Then Fief, Whitney, and Sesapa dove under the wagon to escape the bruising ice stones.

Taterhead and I mounted Sassy and Buster and led the other two horses in a dead run toward a scraggly cluster of trees along a hillside. Lightning can strike trees, but I preferred those odds to being stoned to death. The ride through the hailstones was brutal. I had traded my dress for the comfort of jeans on this leg of the journey, but my bonnet must be back in Fort Kearny by now.

The ice stones were the size of baseballs and felt like bullets. We finally reached the grove and took shelter while the clouds chunked everything they had at us for another ten minutes. Then, as suddenly as it started, it stopped.

Taterhead had kept his arm around Sassy the whole time to calm her. You've got to love an aimless old wanderer like that.

We rode back to check on the others. They had crawled out from under the wagon to look for us and were relieved to see we were okay. We even stood a moment to admire an amazing double rainbow arched across the sky.

The next day, we were only an hour down the trail when the horizon went black with a massive buffalo herd crossing in the distance. Thunder from their hooves caused the ground to shake beneath us.

Taterhead said they weren't likely to turn toward us. Good to know, since being trampled to death wasn't on my bucket list. The tater man took a nap while we waited three or four hours for them to pass…hundreds of thousands of them!

Fief sat, amazed at this massive herd of creatures and the immense prairie itself.

"Who knew all of this land would someday be part of America!" he exclaimed.

"Thomas Jefferson bought it from France—part of the Louisiana Purchase," Whitney said.

Sesapa scoffed. "It didn't belong to him *or* France. It belongs to the Creator and to all who live on it—the rabbits, the elk, the buffalo, and the First People. But it was taken from all who called it home, piece by piece— like Slimrod stole that jewelry."

Fief listened soberly. "I should read up on some of this."

"Good idea," I said. "Whitney probably has a book on it in her backpack."

"No," Whitney retorted. "But I have some air if you need any more in your head."

It didn't take long for the prairie to dry out after the storm, so we gathered more buffalo chips. While I worked as a human pooper-scooper, I wondered about Slimewad. There was something he'd reminded me of…a hawk, maybe? Or some villain I'd seen in a movie?

Before I could decide, a droning noise met my ears. I turned to see a buzzing black cloud of insects slowly making their way toward us. Turns out we weren't the only ones collecting buffalo dung. They were dung beetles. A million of them! But they weren't interested in *our* buffalo chips. They wanted the fresh stuff, so they kept moving toward the buffalo herd.

When the herd finally passed, we moved on to a fork in the Platte River—our first river crossing.

Whitney had mentioned the danger. Now, staring at the cold, fast-moving waters swollen by the recent rain, my speeding pulse rate confirmed that fear.

Taterhead was all business, but so was the river. They had met each other here before.

"The horses don't look too eager to dive in," I said.

"Me neither, but I ain't a horse," Taterhead drawled. "They'll manage—horses are like a harmonica; you just have to know how to play 'em."

Something was always like something to Taterhead.

"The important thing is to keep 'em moving once they start across because the bottom is like quicksand. But if they keep plugging, we'll make it through," the old trader said.

Quicksand! I didn't like the sound of that. I'd seen movies where some poor fool got sucked in and drowned…or was it suffocated? Something unpleasant.

"My job is to keep them horses movin'. Yours is to stay in the wagon and pray," Taterhead shouted.

Our part seemed simple enough until the horses plunged into the water. I felt the wagon shift to a steep downhill angle. What I couldn't feel was my arm. Whitney had grabbed hold of it so tight it was losing all sensation.

Suddenly we heard, "Stop! Stop! I can't swim!"

That's when Slimrod Rumpwrath came spluttering out from underneath the wagon. I couldn't believe it. But there he was! He tried to climb the muddy bank but slipped back into the water. Unable to swim or gain any traction, we watched Rumpwrath get carried downstream by the swift current.

I was too dumbfounded to move, but Fief jumped into the cold, rushing water and swam toward the terrified twit. Taterhead was still trying to keep the horses moving through the riverbed, but they were so startled by Slimrod's commotion that Buster tried to turn back.

That's when the wagon began to overturn. Whitney, Sesapa, and I lunged to one side of the wagon to shift the weight. I saw Fief reach Slimrod and tow him toward the opposite bank. But the wagon continued to tip.

As a last-ditch effort, Whitney threw herself over the side of the wagon and held on, using all of her weight to try and reverse the tilt.

Sesapa untied the sacred bundle from her belt and handed it to me. Without a word, she jumped into the river and swam to Buster to pull him in the right direction, but I could see she needed help.

I tucked Sesapa's pouch under the tarp and dove in the river to help guide the horses toward the far bank while Whitney continued hanging over the side of the wagon to balance the weight. With all that and Taterhead's skillful handling of the reins, horses and wagon finally reached the other side.

As Whitney, Sesapa, and I collapsed on the bank, Taterhead jumped down and gave Sassy a wet hug. "I know'd you could do it, girl. I just know'd it!"

I searched the riverbank where I'd last seen Fief and Slimrod. In horror, I realized that Fief, after depositing Slimrod on the bank, had been unable to drag himself out of the water. He was being swept farther downstream while Slimrod stood there watching us!

"The current has Fief!" I yelled. Whitney, Sesapa, and I sprinted along the bank desperately looking for him. I finally spotted him at a bend in the river, where his lifeless body had become tangled in the reeds.

30
Another Higglby

Whitney, Sesapa, and I raced to where Fief was lying facedown in the river wash. We pulled him onto the bank, then I turned him on his back and gave him five quick breaths of air. Nothing.

"We must keep his soul alive, or he'll disappear forever," Sesapa warned.

Taterhead, not much of a sprinter, finally arrived as I started chest compressions on Fief while counting to thirty. Then, on cue, Whitney breathed two short breaths into his mouth and lungs. We tried again…and a third time.

Finally, Fief's eyes flew open, and he coughed. Sesapa took a deep sigh of relief.

"I better get back and make sure that wagon axle's okay," Taterhead said, then looked around for Rumpwrath. "Looks like that no-good has run off again."

The rest of us waited for Fief to quit throwing up and regain some strength.

Then Sesapa remembered. "My bundle!"

"It's safe," I said. "I'll show you."

We left Whitney with Fief and made our way back to the wagon. Much to our surprise, Slimewad was there with Taterhead.

"Guess he figured it was us or let that wagon train catch him," Taterhead snorted.

I pulled Sesapa's pouch from under the canvas and handed it to her. "Not a drop of water on it!" I said proudly.

She thanked me and retied it to her belt. "I didn't mean to panic," she apologized. "It's just, we've come so far…"

Later, Slimewad filled us in on how he'd escaped from the emigrants. Back at Fort Kearny, Taterhead had fastened two brackets underneath the wagon with a board between them to use as a shelf for extra rope. Slimewad had noticed this when he was helping grease the wagon wheel. That's where his skinny frame came in handy. To escape the angry mob, he'd thrown out the rope and squeezed himself into his own little hidey-hole!

"I was sore afraid I'd be found out when I heard you brats run under the wagon to get out of the storm," he sneered.

"I had my eyes closed most of the time," Whitney recalled. "I was too worried about the wagon being struck by lightning to notice anything else."

"Good thing we didn't need that rope you tossed out—at least not yet," Taterhead muttered. "If we come to a deeper river, I'll be using you, Mr. Rumpwrath, as a pole to see how deep the water is—and you'll be going in headfirst."

The trip didn't get any easier the rest of that day. First was a huge hill so steep we walked it to spare the horses. But going downhill was the real torture. All of us, including Slimewad, had to hold on to the wagon to slow its descent. We would have been using ropes except…Slimewad. We finally made it to the bottom where a wooded glade and clean spring water was our reward.

That evening, I really enjoyed our meal. Partly because Fief was still with us, and partly because we'd come close to losing the last of our food supply in the river. It was bacon and beans, but it tasted like Thanksgiving dinner to me.

After viewing it from afar for days, we finally reached a sharp, pointy rock sticking straight up out of the plains.

"There she is—Chimney Rock!" Taterhead whooped.

Sesapa smiled. "My people didn't call it that."

"What did they call it?" Whitney wanted to know.

"Elk penis." Sesapa shrugged. "We had no chimneys."

I saw the Lakota reasoning, but I also understood why the map makers went with "chimney."

After that came the highlight of the trip so far—we dumped Slimewad. When it was time to turn north again, Taterhead stopped the wagon and told him he'd be walking to Scottsbluff from there.

"There's a trading post up the road—belongs to a Frenchman named Robidoux. And I'll give you some advice—if you try to rob *him*, your robbin' days will be over!"

Slimewad began gathering his things, but Taterhead stopped him.

"Hold on there! I reckon you're still owing me."

"You've got the fifty dollars you charged me!" Rumpwrath said indignantly.

"That was before you nearly ruined my good name by stealin' from hardworking folk. If we hadn't caught you, they woulda thought you and me were partners most likely. *And* it was before you threw out my store-bought rope, leavin' me with nothin' to hang you with."

Slimewad started to talk, but Taterhead cut him off.

"*And* it was before you almost let that boy drown after he saved your worthless hide."

"I thought he'd climbed up the bank behind me," Slimewad argued. "I went straightaway to the wagon to help keep it from turning over!"

"Which was all your fault in the first place—thank you for reminding me." Taterhead spit to punctuate the remark.

Slimewad tossed his bag back in the wagon. "Fine! You can have all the elixir I have left."

Taterhead wound up his mouth and sent a big spitball just past Slimewad's ear. "That stuff would probably kill me faster than a two-headed rattlesnake."

"Well, what then?" Slime Boy shouted impatiently.

Taterhead jerked his head toward the banjo in Slimrod's other hand. "That's all you have worth more than the rocks in your head."

"*Now* who's the thief?" Slimewad hissed. He glared at Taterhead, laser-stared the rest of us down, then left without the banjo.

I watched Slimrod Rumpwrath slither down the road, still wondering who he reminded me of—then it came to me! The beady eyes, the hollow forehead. Could it be he was a distant relative of Jonathan Rimroth?

Sesapa now sat in the buckboard seat as the horses started down a less-worn Indian trail—the kind we'd be taking until we reached Beaver Hole.

"How much do you think that banjo's worth?" I shouted as the wagon rattled along on the barely-a-trail.

"To someone who knows how to play it, it's worth maybe fifteen dollars. But I can't—not yet anyway. So it's only worth the price of gettin' rid of him."

"You got the best of that bargain." Fief grinned.

Taterhead nodded. "Ain't nobody ever bested me in a deal yet. And nobody ever will! Not ol' On-Time Taterhead Higglby!"

Higglby?! There was a silence in the wagon as thick as yesterday's gravy. It was broken by an uproarious laugh coming from the only one in the wagon who wasn't a Higglby... Whitney.

"What's wrong with her?" Taterhead asked.

"She's just glad Mr. Rumpwrath left," I ad-libbed.

"Me too!" Taterhead agreed, then broke into one of his patented songs.

> "Oh, I sure am glad that fool is gone,
> It took him way too long, long, long..."

Taterhead continued to sing, paying no attention to the confab in the back of his wagon.

"I thought the professor said that Higglbys couldn't run into other Higglbys outside the tree because of a magnet or something," Fief whispered.

"He said we couldn't run into anyone we would've known when we were alive," I explained, as much to myself as him.

Whatever the explanation, we decided it was best not to mention our last name to Taterhead. It might lead to embarrassing questions.

We moved deeper into hilly, wooded country. Sesapa seemed to get prettier, if that was possible, the closer we got to the Black Hills. Then she saw some Lakota men watching us from a hilltop.

"We are very near Beaver Hole," she said excitedly.

The farther down the trail we got, the more isolated I began to feel.

"I'm scared," I whispered to Whitney.

"It's because you're in a country surrounded by people who aren't like you and who aren't sure they want you around… welcome to *my* life."

She nailed it. Except for Sesapa, we were the only people for miles around who weren't Indian. *We* were now the *other*. But coming to grips with Whitney's world, and my near-sighted behavior concerning it, wasn't making me feel any safer.

"Taterhead, are there any other white people around here?" I asked.

"Probably some up in the hills. They ain't supposed to be there because it's Indian land by treaty. But there's rumors of gold up there. And there ain't nothin' can keep a white man away from a pot o' gold except a bigger pot o' gold."

A half dozen Lakota men on horseback rode out of the trees some fifty yards away. Taterhead halted the horses.

Sesapa stood up in the wagon and made hand gestures to the men. They returned some gestures and melted back into the forest. Minutes later, we wound around a ridge and peered down into a valley.

An entire village lay before us. Dozens of tipis—tents shaped like upside-down cones—stretched out for half a mile. Sesapa let out a gasp when she saw them, then began to sob.

"It has been so long. It has been so long…"

As the wagon groaned to a halt at the bottom of the trail, I watched Sesapa dry her tears using the palms of her hands and wondered if that was the Lakota way.

31

Visitors

"Look at all them teepees!" Taterhead exclaimed.

"The entrance to a Lakota village always faces east to honor the rising sun," Sesapa explained as she soaked it all in. "Any visitor who enters elsewhere is considered hostile."

"Then east it is," Taterhead declared.

Sesapa also explained that, to the Lakota, things that were round were sacred. That was why their camps were in a circle and why tipis were circular.

"I never heard of a shape being sacred," I said, thinking out loud.

"You've never heard of a cross?" Sesapa answered. "That shape is sacred to some. To us, the earth, sun, and moon, which are round, are holy. Without them, nothing could exist. Should they not be thought of as sacred?"

My ego began shrinking in my head like a turtle into its shell.

"How long does it take to set up a tipi?" Fief asked.

"It only takes the women a few minutes."

"The women?" Fief exclaimed.

Sesapa nodded. "Women are in charge of the tipis and everything in them. They are designed to put up and take down quickly. You can't follow the buffalo and stay in one place."

Four Lakota men riding horses almost as gorgeous as they were, dismounted and escorted us into the village. These guys were tall, good-looking mega-hunks. They obviously didn't like wearing shirts. And they obviously didn't sit around eating Double Stuf Oreos.

Their black hair was shoulder length, sometimes twisted into braids. But since neither the guys nor the horses gave me a second look, I turned my attention elsewhere.

The women were busy all over the place—cooking, gathering firewood, making baskets, you name it. Boys were running races and playing games with bows and arrows. But most of the girls were working alongside their mothers.

Some women greeted us wearing wing-sleeved deerskin dresses with buckskin leggings under their skirts like Sesapa was wearing. Sesapa told them Taterhead was here to trade for hides and pelts. We were told that most of the men were out hunting, so Taterhead would have to wait.

I was in a hurry to get to that grandfather mountain. Since Taterhead was our ride back to Fort Kearny, he might not want to wait for us. But Sesapa was drawn to the village like a bee to honey, so I kept quiet.

Whitney was also enthralled with the camp—she had her sketch pad out. And Fief was soon trying to best a kid half his age at hitting a distant pine cone with a bow and arrow. Fief lost.

Sesapa ushered me into a tipi where a woman offered us buffalo hides to sit on. She greeted Sesapa, then they just sat there. I finally whispered, "Is she mad at us?"

Sesapa shook her head. "It's good manners to stay silent awhile. It keeps us mindful that thought should come before speech."

Great! Something else I wasn't good at.

The woman offered us the tent, and Sesapa thanked her. When the woman left, I flopped down on the buffalo skin. Sesapa said if the tent flap was open, it meant people were welcome to enter. There was also a flap at the top of the tipi to help circulate the air. I left them both open and lay there admiring this mobile home.

I thought about my room in Wendom Hills. I was too tired to miss my TV, or computer, or my phone. But I would've killed for a hot shower and a flush toilet. You don't realize what the real luxuries in life are until your only bathroom is tall prairie grass, and the only thing to bathe in is your own sweat. I fell into a deep sleep until Whitney shook me awake for dinner.

Outside, women were cooking over fire pits while the younger girls brought water and firewood. For us, they ladled out bowls of boiled buffalo stew. I took a bite. To my relief, it wasn't bad, since there are few things ruder than a gag reflex at a dinner party.

Then I saw a woman dump some crickets into the fire. She roasted them until they popped like corn, then she stirred them into a pancake batter. Whitney, feeling the same reluctance I was, watched me take a bite.

"How is it?" she asked.

"Not exactly Cheetos, but do have some." I smiled and filled her bowl.

Taterhead was sitting with some of the older men who had stayed in camp. While the men sat laughing and telling stories, the women worked. One scraped hair off one side of a buffalo hide and flesh off the other. Watching this animal being disassembled in front of me didn't make eating what was probably its innards any easier.

"Tatanka is our word for buffalo," Sesapa explained. "When we kill one, we thank it for its sacrifice. Almost everything you see around you is a gift from tatanka."

She informed us the spoons and cups were made from buffalo horns, the hides were used for shirts, belts, and tipi covers. The brains were smeared on the hides to make them soft for bags and moccasins. The stomach was cleaned out, and *voilà!* A water bag.

Everything of tatanka's was shared: food, clothing, rope, toys, soap, blankets, sewing thread, and hunting bows. Rawhide was boiled into glue to make splints for broken bones, tails were used as flyswatters and ornaments. In winter, the kids turned the ribs into sleds.

"We carve the other bones into arrowheads, needles, and dice," Sesapa added.

"Dice?" I asked.

She nodded. "The men like to gamble—sometimes late into the night."

To Taterhead's delight, the hunters returned that evening with elk, deer, and antelope hides. The success of the hunt called for celebration, so that night the party began. Drums were played, prayers were prayed, songs were chanted, dances were danced.

I had taught Taterhead the three chords I knew from guitar lessons. So while Sesapa played a flute made from a deer horn and I played a drum, Taterhead strummed his newly gifted banjo and sang:

> *"Jingle bells, the river swells,*
> *The gopher's gone to ground;*
> *Gonna grin while I whirl and spin*
> *'Til the hole in my head makes a whistling sound.*
>
> *Butterflies have wings that flitter;*
> *Hawks have wings that flare;*
> *Bedbugs ain't got wings at all,*
> *But my blankets just don't care."*

Even after that song, the Lakota let us stay the night.

Fief and Taterhead slept outside on buffalo hides. But sleep didn't come easy inside our tipi. The one next door must've had an "Open All Night" sign hanging on the flap. There was nonstop chanting, drumming, and gambling.

"What are they gambling with?" I asked, realizing they didn't traffic in gold or silver.

"Anything that's theirs," Sesapa sighed. "Ornaments, their weapons, even their horses."

I thought about Grace. I wouldn't risk her on a roll of the dice. I wished I could hug her right now to help me fall asleep. But no hug, and no sleep. The gambling went on until dawn.

I had barely dozed off when sunlight found the open flap and the side of my face. I smelled smoke rising from the fire pits as the women started breakfast. Then I heard a ripping noise. Sesapa was tearing up the dress Fief had bought that she never wore.

"Hey, we still might need that," I scolded.

"Someone else needs it more," she said.

Apparently, the Lakota men weren't the only ones gambling last night. Fief had joined the fun and lost his shirt—literally. Sesapa was making him a new one from the dress material.

"They don't even wear shirts. Why would they want his?" I asked.

Sesapa smiled. "They wear them in winter. And all cloth is valuable."

I gazed into Whitney's compact mirror. After my bonnet blew to bonnet heaven in the hailstorm, I'd borrowed a hat from Taterhead to keep me from sunburning. It didn't work. I looked like a barbecued potato chip.

Whitney was busy twisting some of her hair into braids. Not to be outdone, I ran a comb through my hair. Sesapa offered me a brush made with porcupine quills. I remembered the bead-and-buckskin doll she'd shown me in the tree. She'd used those quills for decoration, but they worked pretty darn well on tangles too.

Fief stuck his head inside the tipi. I could see he was, indeed, shirtless.

"Did you find me another shirt?" he asked, red-faced. Not as red-faced as I was from the prairie sun, but who could be?

"I'm making one," Sesapa told him.

He looked at the material and recognized the dress.

"I'll not wear that! First you make me buy dresses. Now you want me to wear one?"

"Serves you right for gambling," Whitney said with a smirk.

"I'd never gambled before," Fief sulked. "If I hadn't left my tool belt with Taterhead, I would have lost it too!"

We heard a commotion in camp and scurried out to see what was going on.

Three men had arrived in the village. One of them couldn't have been more than sixteen. He was different from the rest—he had sandy hair, hazel eyes, and a lighter complexion than most Lakota. The three men disappeared into a large tipi they called the council lodge.

"The young one wears two red-tailed hawk feathers awarded for leadership," Sesapa said. "They called him Curly."

Whitney wrinkled her forehead. "I think I read about him in American History."

"American History isn't until next year," I said.

"Honors class," she reminded me. "I think that was what they called Crazy Horse."

"Oh jeez," I whimpered. "You study history *and* remember it?"

Whitney grabbed her sketch pad. "Even if I'm wrong, he'll make a good drawing."

Before the visitors emerged from the council tipi, Sesapa had turned the dress into a great-looking shirt.

Fief wasn't thrilled, but he put it on. We watched some Lakota men crowd around him, chattering.

Sesapa laughed. "They are envious of you. They want you to gamble *that* shirt."

Fief grinned. "Don't worry. They won't get *this* one."

By the time the visitors emerged from the meeting, the mood of the camp was one of concern. As one visitor spoke, the camp became as still as a painting. He had only said a few words when Sesapa gasped. I nudged her for a translation.

"There's been a battle," she whispered. "Two moons ago, a cow wandered into that young man's camp. They butchered it to feed the village. Thirty soldiers came and killed their chief, so they killed the thirty soldiers. Now the army has ordered all Lakota to go to Fort Laramie. Those who don't will be treated as enemies of the US government."

Then the second visitor spoke as Sesapa translated. "The Grandfather in Washington promised 'as long as the grass shall grow and water flow, the Black Hills will remain Lakota Holy Land.' But there is yellow rock in the mountains—the rock that makes the white man crazy. We leave it because it is good for nothing that is good for the land or our people. But the white man looks for reasons to kill our people for it. Soon more blood will be shed—not because of a cow, but because they want to see us dead. They do not seek justice. They seek our sacred land."

Everyone in camp began to talk among themselves as the visitors left the village. Sesapa put her head in her hands. Whitney had stopped sketching.

"They're expecting genocide," Whitney said.

"What's genocide?" Fief asked.

"It's when a country tries to kill off an entire group of people, usually because of their religion or color of their skin." She turned on her heel and went into the tipi. When I joined her a few minutes later, she was absorbed in a paperback book she'd brought—*History of the Plains Indians*.

"That *was* Crazy Horse. He was at the Grattan Massacre, which started over the killing of a cow." She skimmed the section, then added, "It says he was the only famous chief who never allowed his picture to be taken." She looked up. "Maybe I shouldn't have sketched him."

"A photo isn't the same as a drawing," I said.

"Maybe not. But part of what this trip has taught me is to respect other cultures as much as I would like mine respected."

Suddenly we heard loud shouts from outside, and they didn't sound friendly.

I heard Fief yell, "It's okay! He's with us!"

We ran outside to see none other than Peerless the Plunderer surveying Lakota warriors as they grabbed their bows and arrows.

32
Stolen!

As Peerless reached for his sword, Sesapa flung herself between Peerless and her people and spoke to them. The Lakota lowered their weapons, and we hustled Peerless into our tipi before they had a change of heart.

Sesapa was shaking visibly. "I almost cost you your eternal life!"

Peerless looked down at this small girl, barely eighteen, who also had *her* immortal soul to lose, yet she had thrown herself in front of him without fear.

"I did have me a recollect of my last scrum with pirates," he said. "But you, child…I never saw man nor woman any braver than you."

"I don't feel brave. I feel only fear and sadness for my people." Sesapa touched the bundle tied tightly around her waist. "I was waiting until my eyes saw the Six Grandfathers, but I need a place of solitude now to ask for strength and guidance."

Sesapa squeezed Peerless's hand. "I am so glad you are safe," she said and left the tipi.

Whitney looked worried. "The situation here is growing serious. We need to get to that mountain so we can start back to Fort Kearny."

"That's what I come to tell you!" Peerless barked. "I've found a closer knothole. The entrance is only a short trek away."

"Why would there be a tree entrance around here?" I asked.

Peerless shrugged. "Some Higglby died here."

"Maybe it was Taterhead," I said sadly.

"Or…you." Whitney choked.

That was not a comforting thought. Just then, Taterhead stuck his head into the tent.

"What them Indians said sounds like a whole peck of trouble brewing. I'm gonna skedaddle today. Anyone going with me, get packin'."

"We don't need a ride back," Fief said. "We're going back with this man. He's—"

"Our father," I jumped in.

Peerless was as startled to hear that as we were.

"Remember? We told you he was a trapper like you," I said, mainly for Peerless to hear. "We're going to live with him in…" I had no idea how to finish that sentence.

"Oregon, didn't you say?" Whitney answered, looking at Peerless.

Peerless looked at Taterhead. "What she said," he barked, then slammed his mouth shut like a vault door.

Taterhead scratched at his bristle of a beard. "Suit yourself. The wagon's hitched, and I'm a-leavin'. Luck to ya," he said and left the tipi.

Taterhead wasn't good at saying goodbye. Neither was I, but I ran out to where he'd left the wagon. Taterhead was just standing there. When he saw me, he looked off in the distance to nowhere.

"I warn't cut out for married life. I'm a travelin' man. But if I had settled down and had me a passel of brats, I'd want 'em to be like the boy and you three gals."

I reached up and hugged him. "You're like family to us, too, Taterhead. We'll see you again. Trust me when I say this…we *will* see you again."

He managed a smile. "Don't be hanging around here long, ya hear? There's gonna be trouble sure."

With that, On-Time Taterhead climbed on the wagon and gave me a wave. I listened to the clip-clop of Sassy and the gang as they rode away from the village and us.

Between very little sleep last night and all the excitement today, it took my last ounce of energy to drag myself back to the tipi and collapse on the buffalo-skin bed. But as I did, Sesapa ran in clutching the bundle, with tears in her eyes.

"The white buffalo stone…it's gone!"

"Gone? It can't be!" Fief argued. "Unless it fell out of your pouch somewhere along the trail."

Sesapa shook her head. "Someone stole it. They replaced it with this." She opened her palm and showed us a rock—just a plain old rock that had been left in its place.

33

Questions

"How could anyone have taken it?" I asked. "You never let that pouch out of your sight."

"Only that day at the river when I gave it to you," Sesapa said.

Peerless stared at me, furrowing his already well-furrowed brow. "*You* took her buffalo?"

"Of course not!" I snapped. "I hid the pouch under the canvas before I jumped into the river. I was the only one in the wagon, and the bundle was right there when we came back."

"I know it wasn't you," Sesapa wept.

"It had to be that thief, Rumpwrath!" Whitney reasoned.

Sesapa shook her head. "He was never anywhere near me. Besides, to him it would not have looked like something worth stealing."

"You think it was Taterhead?" Fief asked reluctantly.

I remembered the night I saw him rummaging through the wagon. He said he was looking for a bedroll, but he asked about Sesapa's bundle. I swallowed a boulder forming in my throat.

"I did see him poking around our things the first night out," I said reluctantly.

"And you're just now telling us?" Whitney asked.

"I thought he was just being nosy—and I still do. He saw how protective Sesapa was of the bundle, so he thought she might have something he could trade for."

"Then why sneak around?" Fief asked.

"Because he doesn't like to be bested in a trade."

"So only you and the wagon man were alone with the stone, but you say *he* didn't take it?" asked Peerless, plunderer-at-law.

By now, *I* was beginning to suspect me. I knew I didn't do it, but I felt bad Taterhead wasn't here to defend himself.

"That day at the river, Rumpwrath was at the wagon when we went back to get your bundle," I reminded Sesapa.

Whitney shook her head. "Rumpwrath couldn't have found it, decided to steal it, then searched for a stone to replace it with right after almost drowning. He wouldn't have had the time or the gumption."

"Then Taterhead didn't have time either," I declared triumphantly before realizing that made me the chief suspect again.

Peerless stood up. "Whoever did it, the deed is done. It's time to get back to the tree!"

"Peerless is right," Sesapa said. "You're in danger here. You have brought me this far, and I am deeply thankful. But the rest I will do alone."

I shook my head. "We came here to help you, so I'm staying."

"Same here," Whitney agreed.

Fief stood up. "I'm certainly not letting you girls go alone."

"Then it's settled," I said before anyone changed their mind. "We'll need four horses to get us to the mountain."

"Wait, we have to *ride* there?" Whitney panicked.

"It would take too long to walk," Sesapa said. "On horseback, we'll be back by tomorrow."

"Then you'll only need three horses," Whitney said. "You aren't getting me on one of those creatures."

"Okay, you can stay here in camp with Peerless."

"Who says Peerless is staying here?" Peerless roared. "I plan to sleep tonight in the safety of the tree."

"But you're the only one who can take us to the new knothole," I reminded him. "And you wouldn't leave Whitney here alone, would you?"

Instead of answering, Peerless's nose began to twitch. He followed it out of the tipi to a fire pit where a woman was cooking. She smiled and offered him a bowl of fresh boiled buffalo. Peerless took a big bite, and his whole head lit up.

"This is the best meal I've had since…ever!"

Sesapa translated that to the woman. She looked incredibly pleased and offered us each a bowl of something.

"She hopes you like this too," Sesapa translated. "It's snake meat."

Too late for me—it was already in my mouth. I swallowed it with a grimace that I hoped looked like a smile.

But Peerless was in heaven. "Best snake I've had since we raided Ireland."

"Ireland doesn't have snakes," Whitney informed him.

"I know that! I took one with me." Peerless burped.

He was looking for seconds. I was not. I'm all for learning to kill my own snakes, but nobody said I had to eat one.

We heard Fief trying to barter with a guy named Hotah for a horse. Hotah was wearing Fief's old shirt.

"I don't have anything he wants to trade for," Fief muttered.

"That's because he won it all from you last night," I said.

Whitney started back to the tipi. "Maybe I have something."

I gave the rest of my lunch to Peerless and followed her into the tent. Whitney pulled a pair of binoculars out of her backpack.

"We might need these," she decided. She dug deeper and came up a magnifying glass. "This might work."

We took it over to Hotah. Whitney pointed to a gnat on my arm and kept me from swatting it until Hotah saw it through the glass. He gasped. He wanted that magnifier, but Whitney held up three fingers.

"Three horses," she said.

Hotah shook his head. "One," he gestured.

Fief gestured, "Two more horses if I can hit that pine cone with a bow and arrow."

Hotah obviously didn't think much of Fief's ability to win a bet of any kind. He nodded and handed Fief a bow and arrow.

"I get three tries," Fief added.

Hotah shook his head and held up two fingers. Fief nodded.

Fief lined his shoulders up with the pine cone on the ground some fifty feet away and fixed the arrow on the bowstring. He sighted the pine cone, drew back the string, and let the arrow fly. It may still be flying. He missed.

"You said you'd learned your lesson about gambling," I said under my breath.

"I did," Fief said under his. He fixed the bow in position, took aim, and fired again. *Thwump!* The pine cone flew three feet in the air!

"I didn't spend *all* last night rolling dice." Fief grinned. "Half the night I spent practicing archery...shirtless!"

Fief must have a little Taterhead blood in him. He certainly got the best of that deal.

As Sesapa and I readied for the trip, Whitney came to the tipi to say goodbye.

"Is Peerless staying in camp?" I asked.

"Are you kidding? You couldn't pry him away from the home cooking around here." Then she turned to Sesapa. "I don't know if Crazy Horse would approve of my sketch, so I don't feel right keeping it without his permission."

Sesapa thought for a moment. "I was told that some in his tribe spoke ill of him because he was paler of skin than they were. But his father told him the Great Spirit sees a man by his goodness, his courage, and his deeds, untouched by the talk of foolish ones."

Reverse racism, I thought, but Sesapa wasn't through.

"I believe Crazy Horse to be an honorable man filled with greatness for his people. May I put your sketch in the sacred bundle? Perhaps it will fill part of the loss of the white buffalo."

Whitney's eyes watered. "I'd be honored" was all she could manage and handed Sesapa the drawing.

We said goodbye to Peerless and Whitney, mounted our horses, and were on our way to what Sesapa called Paha Sapa... the Black Hills.

34
The Six Grandfathers

The small, sturdy Lakota horses were actually ponies, which made them more comfortable to ride bareback. I had picked a Spanish mustang, white and tan, with an easy gait.

Fief took bearings with Whitney's trusty compass and map every time we stopped to rest the horses. Sesapa giggled at Fief's fascination with the compass.

"In spring, when my tribe would leave the hills to follow the buffalo, we needed no compass because the path we followed formed the shape of a buffalo's head."

After bounding along with the elk a few miles, the scenery changed. Streams snaked around canyons while sunlight bounced off the rippling water, making it sparkle like diamonds. The hills kept rising, each one outgrowing the next. At one point, far below us, a group of buffalo-skin tipis signaled another Lakota camp.

Night falls quickly in the mountains, so we soon made our own camp. Fief got a small fire going. No need for buffalo chips here. Pine trees were everywhere. We dined on buffalo jerky made with dried meat and chokecherries. Afterward, I listened to the crackle of the fire while its smoke had a sleepover in my clothes. When I took off my boots and socks to rub my feet, Sesapa laughed.

"You have feet like mine."

"Yeah, we both have two."

"You have very high arches…and this." She pointed to an extra ridge running down the outside of her foot. She was right. I had that, but I'd never noticed it before.

"You both have almond-shaped eyes too," Fief added. "All the Lakota have eyes like that—except Kit's are Higglby green."

I tried to sleep but could only lie there listening to the night sounds of the forest. The wind whistled eerie tunes through the pines that sounded a little like Sesapa's horn flute.

Just then, the shriek of a cougar filled the canyon. If you ever hear that sound, you'll never forget it. It's freakish—like a crazed woman screaming. This one's unholy shrill bounced off the canyon walls and echoed through the cosmos.

"Welcome to the wild west," I said out loud.

Sesapa chuckled. "I never think of the plains or forests as wild. Only the white man sees nature as something that must be tamed instead of enjoyed. If they could only understand that we belong to the earth. The earth does not belong to us.

"Nature is a blessing to wrap ourselves in. The hills, the forest, the animals—that is what makes a Lakota's heart beat. When you take yourself away from it—or it is taken away from you, the heartbeat fades."

Fief was as awed as Sesapa. "I've never seen wilderness like this. London had more people than you have buffalo. So many that parents couldn't feed their own children."

"Is that what happened to you?" I asked.

"I think so. When I was six, they sold me into servitude for ten years to a man who sailed here to the colonies and taught me a trade. But he was no father. And carpentry is no mother."

"You're part of the tree now," I said. "Why don't you find your parents and talk to them?"

"I get lost too easily. Besides, I'm not sure I *want* to see them."

"We could go with you," I said, hoping to cheer him up.

"Maybe," he said. "I'll think about it." With that, Fief's brash, adventurous soul dissolved into childlike slumber.

I watched Sesapa trace a big circle of stars with her finger.

"These mountains are a mirror of the heavens above them. That shape in those stars is the same shape as the Black Hills. As the sun moves counterclockwise through the constellations, the Lakota move clockwise through the Black Hills from one ceremonial site to another. Each site matches a star in the constellation. The sky map is identical to our earth map."

That was another "wow" file to store in my brain. I went to sleep feeling safer under that celestial circle. But I woke up feeling like one big sore muscle. Riding bareback another day was going to be torture. It was then I noticed the entire mountain was wrapped in a thick fog. Gray gloom blotted out everything more than a few feet away.

I was sure we'd have to wait until the gray wall lifted. But Fief had triangulated our position on the map and thought we could continue if we went slow and worked together.

When it was time to mount our horses, I realized Fief was in more pain than I was. He wasn't used to riding a horse, saddle or no saddle.

"I feel like my legs have been strapped to a barrel," he groaned.

"You'll be fine," I encouraged him. "Just remember, you'll feel twice as bad tomorrow."

The sound I made as I swung a leg over my horse put a cougar's screech to shame, but I put the thought of being bowlegged the rest of my life out of my mind and rode on.

There was no letup in the fog all morning. At one point, Fief stopped to recheck his bearings. He spread the map on the ground, and as I looked at this map of the Black Hills, my jaw dropped. I was staring at the identical formation Sesapa had traced in the sky. They *were* mirror images of each other. As I pondered this silently, Fief pointed the direction, and we powered on.

Finally, the fog lifted and a giant mountain appeared from out of the mist. Sesapa made an audible gasp as she recognized the Six Grandfathers.

"We are here!" she cried.

We gave her a minute to take it all in. It was like she was seeing a long-lost relative. But all I saw was a big mountain.

"Where are the grandfathers?" I asked sheepishly.

She pointed to six columns in the mountain like she was slicing bread. "Those are the six deities responsible for Lakota creation—North, South, East, West, Sky, and Earth. All full of wisdom like our human grandfathers. They are Paha Sapa—'the heart of everything that is.'"

We left the horses below and ascended on foot along with bighorn sheep staring us down every step of the way. Sesapa searched for the best place to leave the tribal bundle—a place where her ancestors and their sacred medicine bag could be together forever. She finally found a crevice in the mountain that extended inward about an arm's length.

"This will be a good place." She smiled.

The ceremony Sesapa needed to offer was meant to be a private affair, so Fief and I left her alone. As we walked away, Fief noticed something off in the distance. He held his thumb in the air and squinted past it.

"Look! If you blot out half of that mountain, the other half looks like two hearts."

I stuck my thumb in the air. He was right.

"I'm surprised you get lost," I said. "You're really good at finding landmarks."

"Maybe I am," he said, holding his head a little higher.

After wandering around on my own, I looked down into a canyon and caught my breath. Running free below me was a herd of wild horses.

As I stood awestruck watching them, an old saying floated through my brain: *The air of heaven is that which blows between a horse's ears.*

I knew I was staring at Grace's ancestors running free in the canyon below. And I could almost feel that air blowing between their ears.

When the horses disappeared from view, I found a rock that made a comfortable chair. As I sat, I saw something shiny next to my foot. I picked it up. It was a gold nugget. I stuck it in my pocket and continued to sit and think.

When I first learned about the sacred bundle, I didn't understand Sesapa's dedication to it. But I'd come to respect and admire its simplicity and beauty.

Then suddenly, I heard the most awesome sound...perfect stillness. Not a buzzing gnat or chirping grasshopper could be heard. A creek below had water so motionless that the reflection of trees in it looked like a still-life painting. Then sounds returned—the flap of wings near a treetop, a porcupine waddling by, the thump of a deer's tiny hooves as it bobbed through the pines like it was playing peekaboo.

The Lakota believe the Black Hills were set aside for the birds and animals—not for humans. Sitting there at that moment, I found it impossible to believe they were wrong.

Other than the white buffalo stone and the sketch of Crazy Horse, Sesapa had never shared what the bundle contained. Whatever it held, I now knew it was more than lucky charms. It was physical representations to her tribe of all things they held dear. Now, as those things were being laid to rest where her tribe had lived, I heard Sesapa's voice carried by the wind.

"I stand on sacred ground—the blood and dust of my ancestors. I thank the sky, the trees, the wind, the rocks, and others who are also my grandparents. I return to you this sacred bundle representing our most important virtues: wisdom, bravery, fortitude, and generosity."

A few minutes later, Sesapa called to us. We made our way down the mountain and started the ride back to camp... much of it in silence.

35

Gone!

Our mission accomplished, we returned to the Lakota village. Now all we had to do was follow Peerless to the knothole, and we'd soon be home.

But I barely managed to swing my pulsating legs from around my horse and onto the ground when I noticed the entire village was being dismantled. Women were taking down the tipis, the men gathering the horses.

"The tribe is moving, but they waited until they spotted you guys on the trail," Whitney said as she and Peerless greeted us.

"Where are they going?" I asked, then felt Sesapa squeeze my arm.

"A place called Blue Water. I spoke to the council before we left. They have agreed to take me with them. Blue Water is where the Brulé tribe is. Hugo and I lived three winters with them after we married. I feel that is where I belong."

How did I not see this coming? Had she been dropping hints all along?

Fief grabbed her by both shoulders. "You have to go back with us, Sesapa. You aren't safe outside the tree."

"He's right," Whitney argued. "You have to come back."

She shook her head. "Whatever happens now, I am prepared to accept. I have never been afraid of going home…only of never really having one.

"Like Fief, I had a brief life. When I died, my thoughts were of Hugo, the one who had saved me. I think that's why my soul transmigrated to the Higglby tree. But now that I have done my best to return the medicine bag to my people, I want to find the Lakota family tree. I feel it will more easily show itself to me here in the land of my birth. Please try to understand. Blue Water is where my heart is taking me."

She hugged each of us, then melted into the hive of activity while we stood there, dumbstruck.

Peerless shook his head and muttered, "She's mad!"

"We can't leave here without her," I insisted.

But Fief shook his head. Fief, the one closest to her age, was also the one closest to understanding her brief life, loss of family so early in life, and the longing for home.

"It's her decision and hers alone," he said.

We gathered our things and walked away. When we reached the edge of the clearing, I looked back. The village was gone.

I tried to force myself to be happy for Sesapa rather than sad for me, but I couldn't shake the sickness I felt leaving her behind—and at such a dangerous time.

To make matters worse, Peerless was having trouble finding the tree, and we were losing the light. I was ready to call it quits when Fief let out a yelp. We followed his gaze. There it was! Our tree.

Peerless tumbled in first, then Fief. I grabbed Whitney's arm, waved goodbye to 1855, and we disappeared through the knothole.

36

Gold Fever

After rumbling through the tree, arguing our location, and changing direction twice, we finally agreed on something— we were hopelessly lost. We decided to exit at the next knothole to get our bearings. So we did.

Wherever we were, it was smelly. I could make out a town in the distance, but its surroundings were anything but a welcome mat. Dead trees, dressed in unsettled dirt and rot, were everywhere. We heard two scruffy-looking miners arguing by a creek not too far away. Neither looked very friendly.

Night was setting in, so we decided on safety in numbers. We'd go to the town and find out where we were and what year it was. Only Peerless was reluctant.

"I wish you'd join us, Peerless," I urged. "You probably fit in here better than the rest of us. You can tell them you're a great buffalo hunter."

Peerless seemed to like that idea but shook his head. "I died in battle once. I'm quittin' while my immortal soul is still intact."

I whispered to Whitney, "Maybe he needs a Higglby cheer."

Whitney thought, then whispered, "How about:

We always stick together because we're Higglbys,
We'll take this town together like we're joined at the knees
Stomp, clap, stomp stomp, clap,
Stomp stomp, clap clap, stomp, clap stomp."

I glared at her. "Maybe something simpler." I turned to the guys. "Okay, Higglbys, it's time for a cheer:

We never give up through thick or through thin!
We never split up and we never give in!"

Peerless and Fief nodded. We did the cheer together, added a low fist bump, and yelled, "*Go-o-o-o, Higglbys!*" And threw our hands in the air. With that, Peerless agreed to join us. He even agreed to leave his helmet and sword behind.

Together, we trudged through the decaying wood to the street of the town. Yes, there was only one street. The first building on it was a saloon. So was the second one.

I was too tired for more sightseeing, so we agreed to find a hotel and wait for morning. We found a sign that said "Lodging" and sent Fief in to get us a room while we waited outside. Peerless was still taking in the sights.

"What's in there?" he asked, pointing to a building where loud music was blaring. Two women—neither wearing the proper ankle-length dress, lounged by the door.

"The sign says 'Hurdy-gurdy House,'" I said.

"Which one of 'em you think is Hurdy?" he asked.

"Hurdy-gurdy is a musical instrument," Whitney informed him. "And I doubt those ladies are musicians."

Fief found a rundown boarding house and scored us a hole-in-the wall room with two beds. The room was dingy and dank, but it was the first bed I'd seen for so long I would have kissed it except for fear of mildew and bedbugs.

The clamor of wagons woke me the next morning. I tiptoed to the window. In the light of day, the buildings looked like something a blindfolded monkey built. Then I saw a sign: Deadwood Stables.

"Deadwood!" I heard myself yelp. That woke up everyone in the room and possibly everywhere in town. I fumbled in Whitney's backpack for her book and found a small paragraph.

"It says Deadwood was named after the dead trees found in its gulch."

"Does it say anything *helpful*?" Whitney coaxed.

"Is this helpful? It was an illegal town built on land in the Black Hills owned by the Lakota Indians and known for its lawlessness and gold miners. Murders were an everyday occurrence."

"Perhaps we should get back to the tree," Fief said.

"Can we at least get something to eat first?" Whitney groaned. "You and Kit must be as hungry as I am, and Peerless hasn't eaten since he ate everything in the Lakota village."

"I only ate what was offered me," Peerless said defiantly. "But I could use more of that back fat and hump meat now."

We left the hotel and started down the ramshackle street, searching for a breakfast nook.

I sniffed the air. "I don't smell any food—unless they're cooking with urine."

A fistfight broke out across the street.

"Peerless, you *do* fit in well here," Fief said with a smirk.

"Better than yourself," Peerless snorted. "Look at ya—still wearing your tool belt. You haven't used it in a month of Sundays or them branches in the tree wouldn't be so muddled up."

"I'd need a tool belt the size of your fat head to fix all the branches in that tree!"

We found a lovely outdoor café with just the right amount of dirt and no tablecloth. Then we dined on a pan full of bacon and eggs, which we ate out of said pan. Fief marveled at a cowboy across the street practicing a quick draw with a gun. When the guy twirled the gun back into his holster, Fief was beyond impressed.

Whitney's mind was elsewhere. "I wish we knew what year we're in," she muttered.

"About a year after these eggs were laid," I said.

Inside the restaurant was a man with a lengthy beard, I'm guessing Merlin the wizard. He was reading a newspaper— the *Black Hills Weekly Pioneer*.

I brightened. "That's what we need!"

Fief followed my gaze and read the newspaper's headline: "'Wild Bill Hickok in Deadwood.' Whose Wild Bill Hickok and why do we need him?"

"Newspapers have dates," I explained. Then I thought about the headline. "I'll be right back."

I'd watched enough western movies with Dad to know Wild Bill Hickok had been a gunfighter that no one would want to go up against. I crossed to the man's table, then leaned in to read the news. Merlin was not amused.

"Get your own paper, you fool kid," he snapped as a gold tooth flashed in his mouth.

"Sorry, sir. Mr. Hickok out there was just wondering what it said." I nodded toward Peerless eating a piece of egg with his knife.

The man gulped. "I don't want no trouble."

He quickly left the paper, the restaurant, maybe even the town. I took the paper to our table and looked at the date.

"It's 1876."

Whitney did the math. "That's only twenty-one years later."

I wasn't listening—a smaller headline on the page had grabbed my attention. It read "Crazy Horse Meeting with Army."

I read aloud: "Rumors abound that Crazy Horse is meeting with Army officials on the Cheyenne River near Deadwood to discuss a treaty. It's the first time Crazy Horse has agreed to talk since the clash between U.S. soldiers and the Sioux Indians in 1855 at Blue Water Creek."

"Blue Water Creek!" Whitney repeated. "That's where Sesapa went!"

I kept reading. "Colonel William Harney's infantry opened fire on the Brulé village with long-range rifles. Eighty-six Indians were killed, seventy women and children were captured, and the village burned. The attack avenged the Grattan Massacre, which started over the death of a cow."

We sat stunned. I flashed back to the women in the Lakota village—the children playing, babies wearing tiny embroidered slippers, the helpful, hardworking women. That vision was now replaced with one of overturned pots and ruined rugs, and bodies strewn between trampled tipis while fleeing women were hunted down like dogs.

"What's all that mean?" asked Peerless.

"It means I'm going to find Crazy Horse," I blurted out. "He was at Blue Water. He may know what happened to Sesapa. If she survived, we can still take her back with us to the tree where she'll be safe."

Fief took out our map and studied it. "The Cheyenne River isn't that far. I'll go with you."

"Okay," I said. "We'll buy two horses."

"With what, your credit card?" Whitney chimed in. "We spent everything we had left on breakfast."

I looked at her. She knew what that look meant and started digging in her backpack.

"Binoculars, Swiss Army knife, and a collapsible cup. Not worth two horses," she said.

"Maybe it is if we add this." I dug into my pocket and fished out the gold nugget I'd found on the Six Grandfathers.

37
The Chase

The stable owner was pitching hay when we entered.
"Whatcha need?" he asked in rhythm with his pitchforking.
"A pair of horses if the price is right," Fief answered.
The stableman sized Fief up. "There's one." He nodded toward a stall.
Even in the dim light, I could tell the horse was old. But the one in the next stall piqued my interest. My avid reading of books about horses was about to pay off. That horse was a paint with "US" branded on him. That meant he'd been a cavalry mount and would be well trained.
"Is this one for sale?" I asked the stableman.
He stopped pitching hay and started pitching a deal. "You like pintos, little girl?"
"He's a paint," I corrected him. "Most paints are pintos, but not all pintos are paints."

The horse blew a gentle puff of air in my face to say hello as I checked his teeth—they wear down from grinding grass and hay—a good indication of how old a horse is. This one was young and looked to be strong.

"He's a good one—name's Dakota," the stableman hyped.

"Then why did the army get rid of him?" Whitney muttered to me.

"They prefer solid-colored horses," I said, glad to be the smart one for a change. "A regiment would have a bay company, a sorrel company, a chestnut company…most of the other colors were considered leftovers. But the color doesn't make the horse."

I turned to the stable owner. "How much?"

As the stableman considered the question, Fief showed him the collapsible cup.

"Ever seen one of these?"

The stableman was intrigued. "Interesting—but it ain't worth no horse."

Fief showed him the binoculars. "How about these? You can spot a fly at fifty paces."

The stableman looked through them. He was more intrigued but handed them back.

"I've seen plenty of flies."

Fief took out the shiny red Swiss Army knife. "Have you seen plenty of these?"

The stableman played with the gadget a few seconds, then said, "All them things will get you one horse, but not two—and no saddle."

I wasn't looking forward to another bareback ride, but we still had the gold nugget. Maybe we could get a second horse and two saddles for that. Fief had the same thought and went out the back of the stable with the stableman to look over the stock in the corral.

Whitney slumped down on a bale of hay in the stall while I put a bridle on Dakota.

Someone entered the stable from the street. "Anybody here?" he yelled.

The voice sounded strangely familiar. I peeked up from behind my horse and there he was! The unmistakable figure of Slimrod Rumpwrath slithering through the door. He was more stoop-shouldered, but twenty years hadn't changed his appearance much, and I doubted it had improved his personality. Whitney and I exchanged glances. She recognized him too.

"He knows us," I whispered to Peerless. "Try to get rid of him."

Rumpwrath started to saddle a horse as Peerless approached. "You a stable boy?" Slimewad asked.

"No, I'm... a great buffalo hunter."

Slimewad stared at Peerless then broke out laughing.

"You're drunk or crazy is what you are, mister. The buffalo are gone. Most all anyway. The army's seen to that. They figured the fastest way to get rid of those murdering redskins was to kill off their food supply."

Slimewad dug in his pocket and pulled out a small leather pouch. "This exquisite specimen is the only buffalo you'll find around here."

A streak of sunlight fell directly on the object. It was the white buffalo stone.

"Beautiful, isn't it?" Slimewad said as he put the stone back in the pouch. "I just sold it to a gentleman from back East. He's waiting for the bank to open."

I had shown Peerless the stone that day in the tree when I returned it to Sesapa. I could tell Peerless recognized it. The only question was, what would Peerless do? Peerless decided to be Peerless.

"I seen that stone afore. You stole it!"

"I did no such thing!" Slimewad shouted. "This has been in my possession for twenty years. It's taken me that long to find a gentleman who recognized its true worth. Two of his associates are on their way here to complete the transaction."

"You stole it!" Peerless repeated. "What's more, you stole it from a Higglby!"

"I did not! I got it off an Indian girl."

"Named Sesapa!" Peerless growled and grabbed the bag from Slimewad. "I told you I was hunting buffalo. Well, this here's the one I've been hunting."

I saw no reason to keep hiding. I stepped from behind my horse. Slimewad had aged a few years, but I hadn't. His eyes almost left his head.

"You!" he hissed. Then he saw Whitney standing beside me. "And you!"

While the Slimer wondered if he was dreaming, Peerless grabbed the pouch and opened it. The buffalo stone fell into his big hand, along with two gold nuggets.

"Those nuggets are mine too!" Rumpwrath yelled. "I need 'em to replace two teeth that got knocked out."

Peerless put the stone and nuggets back in the pouch. "Too bad they ain't already in your mouth so I could knock 'em out again!" he snarled.

Two men on horseback rode into the stable. If they were the men Slimewad was waiting for, something bad was about to happen. They were.

"He's got the stone!" Rumpwrath yelled to the men as he pointed to Peerless.

I did what I do best—panic. I jumped on Dakota's back, grabbed the reins, and turned him toward the stable door.

Whitney, terrified but determined, ran toward the men's horses to push them aside so I could exit. Peerless tossed the stone to her as she sprinted past him. The men wheeled their horses around as I headed Dakota out the stable door.

"Let's go!" I yelled to Whitney.

She hesitated a split second, then hurled herself onto Dakota's back behind me. We galloped off with the two men in hot pursuit.

Whitney was clinging to me like a ferret to a field mouse, but before I could yell "I can't breathe!" I realized I had a bigger problem. A giant tree had fallen across the only road out of town. No wonder they called this place Deadwood!

What's worse, the tree wasn't lying flat. It was leaning against a boulder on the other side of the road. That's when Whitney opened her eyes and saw it too. I know because I heard her scream.

"Hold on," I yelled, "we've got to jump!"

"Do you know how?" asked the terrified voice behind me.

"I don't know!"

I heard Craig's words in my head. *He's the one jumping, not you. Move with his rhythm.*

I moved with Dakota's unrelenting stride. This was a cavalry horse, I reminded myself. They're trained to jump fences and hedgerows. I felt him go airborne and leaned into him, slackened the reins, and before I knew it, we were on the other side. I kept him at full stride as I looked back at our pursuers.

One man had fallen trying to take the jump. The other hadn't even tried.

After a mile or so, I left the path for a patch of woods to give Dakota a breather and see if anyone was following us. Whitney was more than eager to get her feet back on solid ground.

I smiled at her. "You did great, Whit…can I call you Whit?"

"After that ride, you can call me anything you want," she said, still shaking. "That jump! My god, weren't you scared?"

"Is this a bad time to tell you I've been known to wet my pants?"

We half laughed, half cried as we collapsed on the ground.

"Now what?" Whitney asked. "We can't go back to town. Those jerks are still there."

I thought for a moment. "It's twenty years later, but we're still in the Black Hills and not that far from the Six Grandfathers. Why don't we return the buffalo stone to the tribal bundle like Sesapa wanted. Now it's *my* duty."

"Are we close enough to walk?"

"Not yet, but if you want, I'll let you drive."

"No, thank you!" Whitney said.

We climbed back on Dakota's back and headed for the Six Grandfathers.

38
Beyond the Beyond

Each lost in our thoughts, Whitney finally broke the silence.

"I knew about the buffalo almost going extinct—but in such a short time! How can mankind be so heartless?"

"Man has a long way to go before being kind" was all I could say.

We were approaching the Six Grandfathers from a different direction, so I could only hope I would recognize it. We were on a well-worn Indian trail, but I wasn't sure where it led. I scoured the landscape until I finally recognized the rough, ridged stones of the Six Grandfathers. Still, it was a *big* mountain. And I was looking for one little crevice.

I was about to admit the hopelessness of it all when I saw the funny-looking outcropping Fief had pointed out. *If you blot out half of that mountain, the other half looks like two hearts.*

I did, and my thumb confirmed it. On foot, I kept the two hearts to our left until I found the path—then I spotted the crevice.

Sesapa had made it look easy to get to. It wasn't.

"Let me try," Whitney said. Somehow she managed the tricky footing, reached into the crevice, and came out with the bundle. "There's something else in here," she called down.

I was expecting her to pull out a tarantula, but it was a piece of parchment paper wrapped around something. Whitney brought it and the bundle down with her.

Written on the parchment was a note from Sesapa!

My Dearest Kit,

I escaped the massacre and have found my other family tree, which isn't a tree at all. It is a wide, flat hunting ground. I once showed you the doll my grandmother made for me in my likeness. I have made one for you in yours.

Bless you,

Your great-great-ever-so-great-grandmother,

Sesapa

The parchment was wrapped around a bead-and-buckskin doll—a galloping horse with a redheaded girl riding it.

Remembering everything in the bundle was supposed to be wrapped, I folded the parchment paper around the white buffalo stone and returned him to the sacred pouch. I felt an odd sensation as I knotted the bundle…maybe they *had* missed being together where they belonged.

"I think you should be the one to put it back," Whitney said softly.

I nodded. One step at a time, I clawed my way up the slope until I reached the crevice. I remember hearing Sesapa say a few words aloud before she'd left the bundle. So I did too.

"This belongs to a proud Lakota tribe who feared no danger, absorbed many hardships, and remained faithful to their nation, their friends, their family, and their home."

I put the bundle in the crevice and made my way back down the slope.

Whitney had wandered down the mountain while she was waiting for me, so I retraced my steps along the path I had taken when I was waiting for Sesapa some twenty years ago.

The landscape had already changed. Never again would we see wild horses galloping through the canyon. No buffalo-skin tipis marking a Lakota camp, no buffalo to provide the skins, no Lakota to make the tipis.

I found Whitney, and we started down the mountain.

"What should we do with Slimewad's teeth?" Whitney asked. She handed me Slimrod's cloth bag, and I poured out the two gold nuggets.

"For all the gold stolen out of Lakota land, maybe we should put some back," I said.

We buried the nuggets as deep as we could. Not deep enough to never be found again, but deep enough for the earth to know we tried.

We spent the night at the foot of the mountain, then started back to Deadwood the next day. Mid-morning, we stopped to rest Dakota. I found a log and sat down. I hadn't said much since we left the mountain, but I finally had to say something.

"I still wish Sesapa had come back with us. She's one of my grandmothers. She belongs in our tree."

"Her soul was lonely there, Kit. Wherever Grandmama Sheppard's soul is, I hope it's where she's happy."

"Even if it's somewhere you won't be?" I pouted.

"Even if. Sesapa grew up a Plains Indian. This was the world she knew and loved. Shouldn't that be the reward for a life well lived?"

"Don't you ever get sick of being right?" I muttered.

"No—especially when it's you that reminds me I am."

After rummaging through her backpack, Whitney found two energy bars.

"I'll never make fun of anything you have in there ever again." I said almost swallowing mine whole.

Whitney leaned against the log and watched Dakota graze. "I wonder what prehistoric genius first decided to ride one of those," she pondered.

"There weren't any horses in North America until the Spaniards arrived," I reported. "Some got loose or captured and started herds. By then, the Plains Indians knew they could be ridden, so they used them to follow the buffalo and became incredible horsemen."

Whitney stared at me. "So you *do* read!"

"I saw it in a movie—but it was a documentary. What does that tell you?"

"It tells me you're smart but lazy."

"If I were lazy, I would never have picked up buffalo chips."

"*I* picked up most of them—you were just the basket, remember?"

We laughed like you do when you're too tired to think straight. Then the rattle of a wagon got our attention. It was coming from a different trailhead.

An oldish Black man with a loaded wagon stopped when he saw us. "What in tarnation are you two young'uns doing out here alone?"

"We... got lost. Could we ride back to Deadwood with you? She doesn't like horses," I explained with a nod toward Whitney.

"Climb in," he said.

While Whitney gladly got in the wagon, I took off Dakota's bridle and stroked his neck.

"You deserve better than Deadwood, fella. Head for the hills!" I gave him a friendly slap on the rear. He trotted off a few steps, looked at me, then took off running.

"What in the world did you do that for?" the old man asked.

"I'm leaving Deadwood, and he won't fit in my trunk." I didn't mention my trunk was a tree.

Whitney climbed onto the buckboard seat. Her gloating grin indicated I would be riding in coach. I got in the wagon bed and thanked the man for the ride.

"No problem," he said. "My time's my own, and any money I make is more than I made pickin' white man's cotton."

Whitney looked at him curiously. "You were...enslaved?"

"That I was. Half my life. But I'm free now and ain't *never* going back. No, sir!"

"Where are you from?" I asked.

"Born in Virginia—but got sold downriver when I was twelve. They put us in a coffle chained two-by-two. Three hundred of us."

I looked at Whitney who patiently rolled her eyes at my ignorance. "A coffle is a group of animals—or people being treated like animals—chained together in a line."

"You got that right!" he said. "Marched us all the way to Mississippi. Took four months."

"Four months!" I got a little sick in my stomach.

"Did you ever try to escape?" Whitney asked.

"Ran away when I was seventeen. But they found me and whipped me bad." He looked at Whitney. "At least that won't happen to you, child. I finally escaped after the war started—helped recapture the Mississippi River for the Union. Then I changed my name to Eman to let everybody know I'm *eman*cipated." He laughed which, after that story, surprised me.

"I think I'd still be mad," I said.

"I was for quite a spell," Eman admitted. "I vowed to kill me a white man for every time I got whipped. But after the war, I decided I was done with killin'. So I put it all behind me. But it won't never be behind for them slave owners. Every scar on our backs, every slave sold downriver, is a mark on their soul.

"Yes siree, I was done trustin' white folks 'til I finally met me a white man worth knowing. Him and me were partners for a spell. We shared a wagon. That's when I realized I was truly free to go anywhere that pleases me."

That's when Eman broke into a song.

> "Well, I ain't got a dollar, and I ain't got a dime,
> And I ain't got a blanket in the wintertime;
> But I got me a fine horse a-pulling at the wheel
> And there ain't nobody who can best me in a deal."

You will never see two more stunned people than Whitney and I were at that moment.

"Where did you learn that?" I made my mouth say.

"My partner used to sing it. That was fifteen years back—before you were born, I reckon. Then one day, he says, 'Eman, I'm gonna retire.' He gave me everything he had 'cept his old mare and rode off."

"Do you know where he went?" I asked anxiously.

"Wish I did. I think I'm gonna retire too. It's my last trip up here for sure. They're treatin' the land as bad as they treated me. Some men ain't got no respect for nothin'!

And with that, we entered the town of Deadwood.

39
Stablemates

It was night when we pulled in, but darkness only encouraged Deadwood's seedy underbelly. The saloons were loud, and bar fights were scary, especially when they spilled out into the street.

We said goodbye to Eman and went to look for Fief and Peerless where we'd last seen them—at the stable.

And there they were—as glad to see us in one piece as we were to see they had survived Slimewad and the two thugs.

Fief and Peerless had spent the two days working in the stable in return for a stall where they could spend the night.

"But now that you're back with Rumpwrath's gold teeth, we can get us a room." Fief grinned.

"We don't have the teeth anymore…or the horse," I confessed. "So I hope you did a good job cleaning our stall."

Confused, Fief pushed his cowboy hat back, and that's when I saw the bandage.

"What happened to your head?"

"Interesting story, that," Peerless said. "As you two were galloping off yesterday, Fief here comes in and sees me tangling with the two riders. He runs up to help, but one of 'em kicks him in the face. Fief falls against that wood beam and knocks hisself out."

Fief picked up the story. "I came to and saw Peerless trying to stop those two gorillas. But they galloped off after you. That's when I see Rumpwrath sneaking up behind Peerless with a knife in his hand, ready to shiv Peerless in the back."

"Can you believe that?" Peerless cut in. "I turn and see that sneak ready to thrust his dagger, then suddenly his eyes bug out, roll up in his head, and he crumbles to the floor! Fief is standing there instead. He'd thumped Slimy on the pate with his hammer. Then he says to me, 'And *that's* why I always wear a tool belt.' Then he twirls his hammer back into its holster!"

We laughed and talked until Peerless became obsessed with the smell of bratwurst wafting through the stable door. I wanted to buy them a dinner worthy of heroes but remembered we were broke. Then I remembered we weren't.

I pulled the gold nugget I'd forgotten I still had out of my pocket, and we celebrated our last night in the Wild West with the best food we could find in Deadwood—including some ale for Peerless.

We were eating our meal by lantern light in the stall when I remembered Slimewad. "What happened after Fief hit him?" I asked.

"You don't want to hear while you're eating," Fief said. But that didn't stop Peerless.

"I determined it was time to put that backstabber out of his misery for good," he confessed. "So I pulls out my hatchet to separate his neck from his vitals when Fief here stops me. He tells me in some places, if you kill a man, they tie him to you, and you have to lug him around for the rest of eternity! Well, I sure didn't want to be dancing forever with that Rumpscum…"

Peerless stopped to swig some ale, so Fief filled us in.

"Peerless grabbed Slimy by his thieving neck, and says, 'You shall be returned to the womb from whence you came.' Then he picks Slimewad up, dumps him in a big pile of horse plop and says, 'My apologies to the horse.'"

"We saw him leave town on a stage a few hours later," Fief chimed in.

"I hope he bathed first," I said.

"I hope the other passengers held on to their wallets," Whitney fretted. "I still wonder how he got that buffalo stone."

I'd been thinking on that during the ride back with Eman.

"I'm pretty sure it happened at the river," I said. "I remember seeing Rumpwrath watching us from the bank around the time Sesapa gave me the bundle. I think he saw me put the bundle under the canvas, so, while we were busy trying to save Fief, Rumpwrath was busy switching the stones."

Whitney wasn't buying it. "He didn't have time to find a replacement stone. And at first glance, the buffalo stone wouldn't have looked like something worth stealing."

I leaned forward on my bale of hay. "*Unless* he heard us talking that day when we were walking next to the wagon, not knowing he was under it."

Whitney gasped. "You did say something about how much the stone would sell for in New York!"

I nodded. "That gave him plenty of time to plan the switch. He probably took a break from his hidey-hole that night while we were sleeping and found a small rock, hoping for a chance to make the switch."

Whitney grimaced. "To think he was under the wagon with us during that hailstorm."

Fief nodded. "I was more worried about cracking my head on the axle than finding a sneak thief above it. And with all the thunder and pounding of hail, he could've been singing *Yankee Doodle* and we'd never have heard him."

I leaned back. "The important thing is we returned the buffalo stone to its rightful place, got Slimewad to trade two gold teeth for a pile of poop, and we've cleared the good name of On-Time Taterhead Higglby. This calls for a Higglby cheer."

Whitney jumped up and struck a cheerleader pose. "How about this?"

"We've... got...razzmatazz!
And real pizzazz!
Hey, you! Don't make us mad!
'Cause Higglbys got
Razzz...ma...tazzz!"

She threw in cheerleader choreography, shook some booty, then grabbed some hay and tossed it in the air.

"Where did you learn to do that?" I asked.

"And can you do it again?" Fief squeaked, his eyes as big as saucers.

"I'm on the pep squad at school," she told me. "And no," she told Fief.

"I thought you were a science geek," I retorted.

"You and your stereotypes...can't I be both?"

"I guess," I said flatly. "But it seems a little unfair to us mortals."

Peerless was deep in thought. "What's this razzmatazz, and how did we get it?"

"It's like Viking courage," I said.

This pleased him. He stuck his hand out and joined in a rousing *"Go-o-o-o, Higglbys!"*

40
Homecoming

The next morning, we headed for the Higglby tree. For days, I'd been eager to get back, but now I was lagging behind as we made our way to the grove. We had helped Sesapa solve her problem, but going home meant having to deal with some of my own.

Thoughts began to clog my head about the uncertain world I was going back to. The tree had to remain a secret, the town bully would still be out to get me, and the only friend I had left from my childhood was a horse. I glanced up and saw Whitney was waiting for me to catch up.

"Thank you," she said.

"For what?"

"I think the main reason I wanted to come with Sesapa was to get my mind off my loneliness after Grandmama died.

I'll still be lonely, but now I know I can face it. I'm ready to go home."

"I am too. I've got a whole three-part plan to change my image. But afterwards, my dad may hate me."

"Your dad will never hate you, but…"

That "but" didn't sound good.

"I hope you won't end up hating yourself," she finished.

I sneered. "You don't even know what I'm planning…do you?"

"Trying to rebrand yourself with money and prestige?"

"What's wrong with that?" I said flatly. Sometimes I wondered if Whitney wasn't a little envious of me.

"Did you earn either of those things yourself?" she asked.

"What difference does that make?" I barked.

Whitney stopped and looked me in the eye. I hate when someone does that. I always come out second best. But Whitney's voice wasn't lecturing; it was one of concern.

"Money won't change your identity. Only actions can do that. We have to fight to be who we want to be. When I spoke to that wagon train of people, I was lucky they didn't come after me like they did Rumpwrath. But things have to be said before things can get done."

Her answer didn't sound all that envious.

"Okay, so I'm not as brave as you," I blurted out. "We Higglbys have always been cowards."

"Not the ones I've seen. Fief died on his way to fight for his country, and Peerless sailed the high seas and took on all comers before dying in battle. Hugo left civilization to explore unknown territory, then raised two children by himself. So don't blame a name for not facing your problems head-on. Your name is no excuse to let your "best friends" walk all over you, or let your worst enemies toss you in a dumpster and live to tell about it…at least, not with their original teeth in their mouth."

I stopped in my tracks and turned to her. "Whitney Sheppard, you are the most opinionated, headstrong, presumptuous know-it-all I've ever met."

My stare was met with a pair of brown, unblinking, self-assured eyes, but I continued.

"Let me tell *you* something. It wasn't smart to talk back to the daughter of a prominent lawyer who had dared to call you a bike thief. And it wasn't very nice of you to tell me my friends were jerks. And it was downright insane for you to open a dumpster lid expecting a chainsaw murderer to leap out—you're just lucky all you got was me!"

A hint of a smile creased Whitney's lips.

"By the way," I added, "I don't think I ever thanked you for that last one."

"Taking a bath was thanks enough."

"Well, my point is, you aren't always smart. But maybe it is time for me to grow up…and for both of us to go home."

We passed the creek I remembered seeing when we first arrived, and soon caught up to Peerless and Fief because they'd quit walking. Then we saw why. Standing between us and our tree was a huge buffalo.

"What's that?" Peerless asked incredulously.

"A buffalo," I answered.

Peerless looked confused. "I thought a buffalo was tiny and white."

"Not the real ones," I explained.

I felt humbled to be so close to such a grand animal. It was bigger than a grizzly bear and a Clydesdale horse put together. Some shaggy winter hair still clung to his sides, and a beard hung from his chin, giving him an air of ancient wisdom. His nose was the size of a cantaloupe, and his big brown eyes watched us from under two silver-gray horns turned majestically toward the sky. Four little chickadees were hitching a ride on his back.

Peerless took a step back, then I heard *snap!*

Peerless fell to the ground—his foot caught in a steel trap. Fief and Whitney lunged at the contraption to pry the steel jaws apart.

As Peerless stared in horror at his mangled foot, my mind flashed back to my tetanus shot.

"Peerless, if you stare into that buffalo's eye, you can see… Thor."

Thor was all I could think of, but it worked. Peerless quit looking at his foot and fixed his gaze on the buffalo's eye.

Fief and Whitney pulled the trap apart long enough for me to snatch Peerless's foot out before the trap snapped shut. Whitney grabbed her first-aid kit and poured alcohol on the wound. I expected Peerless to send up a howl, but he was still staring at the buffalo's eye as she expertly bandaged his foot. Then Peerless looked at me, awestruck.

"I saw him! And I saw the lightning of his hammer!" Peerless stared at his foot. "He healed me with his hammer!"

"Yeah, his hammer." I turned to smile at Whitney, but she had sprinted to the creek with the trap and hurled it in so it could never be used again. Only then did the buffalo lumber away.

Peerless considered himself healed but leaned heavily on Fief as we hiked into the grove.

"Nice trick you pulled on Peerless," Whitney said. "One Grandmama used to use."

"That's who I got it from," I admitted.

"Then I'd say that makes you an honorary Sheppard." She smiled.

"I'll try to make you proud. Should I think up a cheer?"

"Later," she pleaded.

Then we saw it—the magnificent Higglby tree. Fief and Peerless hobbled toward it like it was a lost puppy. Whitney couldn't see it, but she ran too.

I gave one last look at the man-made travesty that was Deadwood and thought, if land could scream, we'd all be deaf. I grabbed Whitney's arm and we disappeared into the knothole.

Once we were inside the tree, Fief and Whitney offered to make sure the route ahead of us was clear so Peerless wouldn't have to do any extra walking. While we waited for them to return, the wounded Viking studied the confines of the tree.

"I've been sore afraid to leave this tree since my friend was disappeared. But I spent my whole life warring—I raided, I kill't, and I partook of the drink. I once drank a barrel of beer so I could use the barrel to bury my wife."

"You had a wife?" was all I could say to that. "Is she here in the tree?"

"Not after that burial. She's in her tree. Never visits. My point is, I was fearless! I once charged into battle without armor, believing I'd be protected by my fury and rage."

"What battle was that?"

"My last one. But now, after spoiling that Rumpywrath's thieving, and almost being back-knifed, and my foot nigh tore off by an iron jaw, I've been rememberin' the rush of never knowing what the next day will bring. This is who I am!"

"So you're not afraid to leave the tree anymore?"

Peerless nodded. "Thor would want it that way!"

Our next stop on the way home was Hugo's to tell him about Sesapa. But when he saw us, I could tell he already knew.

"She spent her whole life doing for others," Hugo confided to us. "She deserves some time to herself. I'll go to her one day. But for now, she's where she's always dreamed of being—home."

The old Frenchman studied me. "But part of her is still here—you have her cheekbones and her eyes—their color is Higglby green, but their shape is pure Lakota."

After I promised to visit him again soon, we left Hugo and started toward the twenty-first century. At one point, I heard Whitney sigh. "If we do all have trees, I hope everyone in mine is free. It hurts to know some people lived their entire life never having a single day of freedom."

I wondered if she was thinking about Eman and how he was one of the "lucky" ones.

When I saw the old elevator that would take us to the two thousandsies, it was like staring at a hot fudge sundae. But when we piled in, Peerless found a note stuck in the steering wheel.

"What does it say?" I asked.

"It says, 'Blah blah blah blah blah,'" Peerless retorted. "I told Your Highness I can't read."

I took the note. "It's from the Professor. He wants to see me."

Even though no time would have passed when Whitney and I climbed out of the tree, mentally, we had been gone two weeks. I was beyond ready to get home, but I did owe the professor for explaining about my DNA and branchitivity.

When we entered his office, the room was exactly the same. Even the books I'd knocked off the shelf were still lying on the floor. Uncle Elbert looked up as we trudged into the room.

"You wanted to see me?" I prompted.

"Two things!" he said, hunting down a paper on his desk. "I've comprised a list of Higglby characteristics. I know you have green eyes, wild red hair, and three nose freckles. Are you left-handed?"

"Yes."

"Do you have ten toes?"

"Yes."

"Do you have a deviated septum?"

I stared at him.

"Can you breathe out of both of your nose holes?"

"One side gets stopped up a lot."

"Did you suck your thumb as a child?"

I nodded.

"Aha! You are the first green-eyed, left-handed, red-haired, ten-toed, deviated-septumed, three-freckled, thumb-sucking Higglby who's ever existed. That combination may be what triggered a genome in your DNA to allow you to see the tree before your demise."

"There are three more things you might want to check," I suggested. "Almond-shaped eyes, very high arches, and an extra ridge on the outside of my foot."

The professor gasped. "Let me see!"

I bared my foot for him to study.

"Amazing! It's as if such a foot was not meant for a shoe—also, your foot is filthy!"

"You said you had *two* things for her?" Fief reminded him.

"Ah, yes!" Uncle Elbert sauntered to the couch and rolled a bike out from behind it.

I thought it was a new bike. Then I looked closer. It was my old bike, but gleaming with shiny new metal painted a bright red, and the frame was now shaped like a big H.

"You'll find it is almost indestructible!" the professor said. "Judging from the condition it arrived in, I thought that feature advisable."

"You're right about that," I said, daring to dream.

"I also added a security system in case someone tries to pilfer it."

"Great!" I shouted. "If *pilfer* means steal."

He nodded. "It's harmless, but it will give them a bit of a start. This switch activates it."

He pointed out several other upgrades, then I thanked him profusely.

"Glad to be of service," he said and waved us away.

Next stop, the lobby! When we got to the trunk, Whitney went out of the knothole first so I could hand out the bike. But before I could climb out, Peerless had a thought.

"We should do a cheer," he said.

"Okay—but just the last part," I suggested. The three of us touched fists.

"*Go-o-o-o, Higglbys!*" Fief, Peerless and I shouted and threw our hands in the air.

Unfortunately, I raised mine too fast. I lost my balance and fell out of the tree. Next thing I knew, I was in the Forbidden Forest lying flat on the ground.

"You really should work on your landings," Whitney said. She picked up an unopened Pop-Tart she'd left sitting in her bike helmet. "Still untouched—time stood still for us!"

Fief stuck his head out of the tree. "Whitney, I thank you for your help and hope you'll visit again." He smiled nervously, hit his head on the knothole, and disappeared inside the tree.

I grinned. "I think he likes you. Do you like him back?"

"Not like that," Whitney said.

"Why not?" Then I gasped. "Is it because he's white?"

"It's because I'm thirteen and he's a ghost."

"Oh. So you're prejudiced against ghosts?"

I felt a Pop-Tart bounce off my head as we pedaled home.

Killing Snakes

I'd only been gone like an hour in Wilderidge time so no need to greet everyone like a long-lost relative. I casually walked into the farmhouse and found Angie stacking rolls of black-and-yellow wallpaper. I think a Bumblebee Room was about to buzz in.

"Hey, Angie, is Dad out in the junkyard?"

"No, he's at the store. And I wish you wouldn't call it that," she added pleadingly.

That stopped me cold. Suddenly, it did sound like a rotten thing to say.

"You're right. I'm beginning to understand why Dad collects old things. But I'll never like being called an alley cat at school."

Angie shrugged. "An alley cat is a cat that's learned to make its own way in the world. If I were a cat, that's the cat I'd want to be."

Zing! She had a way of looking at things that hit you right between the eyes.

I went to my room and took a much-needed shower. I washed every inch of me, from the top of my head to the bottom of my filthy feet—as noted by the professor. Then I jumped on my tricked-out new bike and cruised into town.

Say what you will about two-hundred-year-old people— the professor knew bikes! It had superior balance and what felt like a hundred gears shifting by themselves. It was like riding a jet plane with pedals.

I saw Crandall's Creamery and decided to celebrate the invention of ice cream. And maybe someone from school would be there to admire my new bike. There was. Unfortunately, it was Jonathan Rimroth!

I started to keep riding until the things Whitney had said about not facing my problems whipsawed through my brain.

When I'd first smarted off to Jonathan, I ducked into the lunchroom. After I'd laughed at the soccer ball double-bouncing on his head, I ran away. But I hadn't seen him since he and Dozer shoved me in that dumpster. Was I really going to just ride away?

I made a sharp turn into the Creamery lot. Jonathan's eyes lit up when he saw my new bike.

"I'd like to take a spin on that!"

"Sorry, it only lets humans ride it," I retorted. I left the bike unlocked, but I activated the "pilfer alarm" in case Rimroth got the urge to take a joyride. Sure enough, I glanced back to see Jonathan reaching for the handlebar. Suddenly, he was launched a foot in the air. When he came down, his hair was standing on end.

I shut off the alarm and jumped on my bike. I pushed the "forward thrust" button and zoomed away. With this new super setting on my bike, I was at the stables before Jonathan knew what zapped him.

Silver Saddles was buzzing with activity.

"Well, look who's here."

I turned to see Creamery Hunk, himself, Craig. "Why all the commotions?" I asked.

"The quarterfinals for jumping are Saturday, remember? I thought maybe you'd enter. Your friends did."

"Not *my* friends! How's Grace?"

Craig's mouth curled into a grin. "She's the best. I've been working her out on the jump course since your mom is still laid up. I was hoping you'd take that part over for me when I leave."

"Leave?"

His grin got bigger. "I got accepted at Amherst."

"Congratulations," I said, my heart withering.

"I got a baseball scholarship; otherwise, I'd be applying at Muckrake U. Want me to saddle Grace for you?"

Saddle! I'd forgotten what one was.

"Sure." I smiled. "I'll meet you at her stall."

I'd been planning to spend some time with Grace, then go back to the tree to visit with Fief and Peerless, but hearing that Craig was leaving made me rethink my plans.

I began to wonder why I was so anxious to get back to the tree. Maybe because I felt special there—me being the first mutant and all. Or maybe it was just a good place to hide.

I remembered what Whitney had said about her honors class that first night we met. She'd been put in a white "boys only" club. But she didn't leave. She leaned into it. She didn't sulk or withdraw; she sucked every inch out of the experience and made it her own. Maybe that's what I needed to do with this mutant thing. Use it to make me bigger, stronger, better.

My brain went into overdrive. Maybe Craig's "kid sister" should leave him something to remember her by.

I made a beeline to the office to check the events list. Valerie and Crystal had signed up for show jumping. How good could I get in four days? Craig had trained Grace; I just needed someone to train me.

I ran to the stalls and, after hugging Grace like I'd never hugged her before, I asked Craig if he would give me some jumping lessons.

"That's not really my job around here…" He looked at me. "Thinking about competing?"

"If I can get good enough not to embarrass myself or Grace."

He looked me over—not like a guy looks a pretty girl over, more like a rancher evaluating a prize steer.

"You been working out?" he asked.

"A little mountain climbing," I confessed. "I think I'd kick myself if I didn't at least try to beat those two Rein Bows…I'll pay you," I added. I admit it felt nice knowing I wouldn't have to unload piss pots to make good on that offer.

Craig narrowed his eyes. "If taking on those two girls is why you want to compete, I'll do it for free."

By the time Grace and I got to the paddock, most of the crowd had left. But as I climbed into an actual saddle, I noticed the girl from the Filly Phosphorescents—the one who owned the paint horse—sitting on the ground, staring at nothing.

"Are you okay?" I asked.

She tried a smile that didn't quite take. "My horse has a bone bruise, so I can't ride him for a few weeks."

"He's a beautiful horse," I said.

She looked surprised. "You know Smokey?"

"I've admired him from afar," I said. "I rode a paint a couple of days ago—a great horse." I didn't mention he was a cavalry horse and had saved my life in Deadwood.

The girl introduced herself as Brenda, then she slumped again. "I was the club's best chance at a trophy."

"Could the Filly Phosphorescents use a new member?"

She looked at me with suspicion. "Aren't you one of the Rein Bows?"

"Not anymore," I reported. "I doubt if I'm good enough to win, but it'll sure make them mad."

"Wow! A Rein Bow riding for us? I can't wait to tell the others!" Brenda jumped up to leave but yelled back, "They'll wet their pants!"

Been there, I thought. My workout with Grace went well. For anyone who wants to get in shape, I highly recommend walking the Oregon Trail, living with the Lakota, hiking the Black Hills, and leaving Deadwood at least once in a dead run.

Afterward, I stopped by to see Mom and make the dreaded announcement that I'd lost the gold watch she'd given me. She didn't look all that surprised.

"I was afraid that might happen. That's why I didn't buy you a Cartier."

When I told her I wanted to enter Grace in a jumping contest, she teared up. "My little girl is jumping. And I won't be there to see it."

"I doubt you'll be missing much, but I'm giving it a try."

I biked back to the antique shop. Dad was with a customer, so I browsed through some out-of-print books on a shelf.

A book called *Gossamer Wings* caught my eye. In it was the poem Mom had mumbled some of the day of her accident.

By firefly light in a star-filled trance,
The clouds will swirl, and the woods will dance.
And I will dream of wonderful things
Like taking flight on gossamer wings.

Flying high where the air is pure,
My thoughts will be clear; my path will be sure
And no one knows sadness; so only rain weeps,
All songs ring with joy, and friends are for keeps.

When the customer left, I took the book to the counter.

"How much?" I asked.

Dad checked the price. "Thirty dollars."

"That's outrageous!"

He looked the book over. "You're right...forty dollars."

"Hmpf! I *was* going to invite you to my first jumping contest at the riding academy."

"For real?" The old quarterback was excited. "In that case, this a gift—unless you win money. Then it's sixty dollars."

"Deal!" I said. "And since there are no cash prizes, thanks for the gift."

42
The Braidy Bunch

Friday afternoon, I was back at Whitney's house. Trissa was straightening my hair again. And again, Branca and Holly stopped by to visit.

Whitney had offered to decorate my helmet for the contest, but I had left it at the stable. She still wasn't a fan of horse flesh, but she agreed to go with me to the stable after Trissa finished my hair.

"You can decorate the helmet while I try to braid Grace's mane," I suggested.

Trissa stopped in mid-comb out. "You're going to braid a horse's mane?"

"Unless I can talk *you* into doing it." Trissa's expression told me she was interested.

Branca eyed Trissa. "You really gonna do that?"

"Why not?" Trissa mused. "It may even go on the top of my résumé—if she wins. Otherwise, I might move it down some."

"This I gotta see," Holly said.

When we got ready to leave, even Branca decided this was too good to miss, so we all biked to Silver Saddles and I introduced them to Grace.

"Good Lord, you're gonna ride that big thing?" Branca asked.

"That's the general idea."

Green and white were the Filly Phosphorescent colors, so Whitney had brought rhinestones and lime-green ribbon to glue on my helmet.

Trissa took the mane braiding very seriously. First, she washed and conditioned Grace's mane, then did a blow-dry.

I was trying on the helmet when Valerie swirled into the stable and bumped into Holly. I assumed Valerie was going to apologize, but when she recovered from the jolt, disgust swept across her face.

"Who let *you* in?" she said to Holly with utter contempt. Then she saw Trissa, Branca, and Whitney. Her jaw fell faster than the Six Flags Drop of Doom.

"Oh my God! There's a whole pack of you!"

Then she saw me.

"I might have known," she hissed, and stormed out of the stable.

I stood like a statue. "I can't believe that," I mumbled.

"I can," Whitney said.

I'd heard that tone from her before—the day I thought she was a bike thief.

I followed Valerie out of the stable. She was next door in the tack room making a call, probably to 911. When she saw me, she stopped.

"Get them out of here, right now!"

I stiffened. "Where exactly does your gall come from—your pasty white face? Your money belongs to your dad. Your grades belong to whoever you cheat off in class. And your morality stinks."

"A Higglby lecturing me?" she spat.

"A proud Higglby. And you might want to think twice about spewing meanness out of every blowhole in your body, Valerie Richardson, because if you ever pull your head out of your bigoted behind, you won't like the welcoming committee. And if you ever insult my friends again, I will hurl you into tomorrow!"

I walked out of the tack room shaking with anger and sick to my stomach—not because of what I said, but because it needed saying, even in this day and time.

I probably hadn't said enough, but how do you talk to a white wall of sublime ignorance? I had invited my friends into Valerie's "for Whites only" world. And if they had dared to defend themselves, the cops might've shown up and...

I felt sick to my stomach again. This time I threw up.

By the time I got back to the stall, Trissa had finished braiding Grace's mane. Grace was always a beautiful horse, but she looked like a professional jumper now.

"Wow, Trissa! You really are good."

"You aren't bad yourself," Trissa said. "These walls are paper thin."

"So is Val's character," I muttered.

"She was doing White math," Branca said. "One black person is an insult. But four is a hostile takeover."

"I wish I'd worn my Black Panther shirt," Holly said with disgust.

"You don't have one," Whitney said.

"It's on my shopping list now." Holly fumed.

I slumped down on a bale of hay. "I probably didn't say everything I should've. I'm ashamed to be white right now."

Whitney took out her phone and scrolled to a picture of a young white woman in a Navy uniform.

"Is that your mom?" I asked.

"White and proud." Whitney smiled.

"I wonder how she would've handled Val," I sighed.

"Probably the same way you did. Or she might've hurled her into tomorrow. Go Navy!"

43
Grace Under Pressure

I got to the stables early the next morning. The jumping arena was modeled after an English countryside. From a distance, it reminded me of a fairy tale. Up close, it was more like a minefield.

One jump looked like a gate, the next like a castle wall, another like a moss-covered fence. There was a hedge that would be tough to jump because it was wide. There were also some bales of hay, and my personal favorite—a big log. Not as big as the tree Dakota jumped, but big. The dazzler was the last jump someone had dubbed "Old Hateful." It was high *and* wide.

There were ten jumps in all. I walked the course making mental notes. The jumps had to be made in the right order and the event was timed, so my head had to be a GPS.

When I got to the last jump, Old Hateful, my heart beat faster. We'd practiced a similar one, but each time it was like doing a loop-the-loop on a roller coaster. Your brain yells, "This is fun!" but your body screams, "How stupid are you?"

A horse can feel a rider's nervousness, so I shooed the butterflies away and headed for the locker room. I pulled on a new pair of bright white stretch pants. I still thought my legs looked like two hockey sticks in a pair of riding boots, so I would have to rely on my inner beauty.

I put on a white shirt, navy blue jacket, and a new pair of riding gloves Mom had bought me—with a subtle warning not to lose them.

Craig had groomed Grace and was busy shining my English saddle to a high gloss.

"A friend of yours came by. She left your helmet," Craig said. Whitney had taken it home to add some finishing touches.

"Love what you did with Grace's mane—and yours," he said, seeing my straightened locks for the first time. Before I could answer, Valerie strode in to get Sheba.

"Well, if it isn't Little Miss *Trés Gauche*."

I looked at Craig. "That means behaving in a socially awkward way...like using French expressions even if you can't find France on a map."

Valerie's eyes locked onto my hair. I'd had my helmet on last night when we tangled, so this was like finding another present under the tree.

"Well, lah-dee-dah! A new hairdo," she snarled. "Who did that for you, one of those—"

"You should watch how you talk," Craig broke in. "We have rules around here."

Val turned on him like a Tasmanian devil. "And one of them is I can have you fired."

Craig smiled. "I don't know how—yesterday was my last day."

"Then what are you doing here?"

Craig rested an arm on Grace's stall and met Valerie's eyes. "Talking to a pretty girl…then you walked in."

He didn't wait to see the red rage filling up Val's face like a pitcher of cherry syrup. He just tipped his cowboy hat and left.

"Mon dieu!" I exclaimed. Then I followed Craig's lead and left.

I led Grace to the warm-up ring and stroked her wine-red neck. "Whatever happens, girl, you're the greatest horse ever!"

She snorted something back at me. I think it was "We've got this."

The crowd was growing bigger and louder as someone pinned number 32 on me. I spotted Brenda, my new Filly Phosphorescent friend, in the crowd and waved. Every parent and kid in a lime-green hat was cheering me on. So were my dad and Angie. Angie even came early to video the event. She majored in communications in college, so video production was still a passion of hers.

Then I saw a shocker. Valerie's mother was there with Jonathan Rimroth Sr., our beloved crooked councilman. I didn't want Grace to see that shame, so I headed in a different direction.

That's when I saw Whitney and the gang. Trissa snapped off some pics. "Win or lose, that horse is definitely going on my résumé," she said proudly. And that's why I'll always love Trissa.

Last night as I was trying to fall asleep, I thought about the Rein Bows—little girls I'd grown up with. The ones who loved horses. But it finally hit me like a brass bat—Valerie didn't love horses; she loved owning one. A horse, to her, was like a designer dress—just an accessory to be admired by her adoring fans. And the three biggest turd-worshippers at her feet had been Blaine and Crystal and me.

But a blow to Val's ego came to light this morning. Crystal had dropped out of the event. Some boy had invited her to a beach party, so that was her passion now.

Halfway through my event, several competitors had already been eliminated. Denise, another Phosphorescent, was one of those. But Valerie had run a clean course. And so had Blaine, although her time was pretty slow.

Now it was my turn. I repeated my mantra: *Keep your rhythm, aim for the center, find the next jump before you hit the ground.*

I focused on the area between Grace's ears as the timekeeper gave me the signal. With a click of my tongue and a touch of my knee, we were off and trotting.

We finished the easy jumps. Then it was time to bear down. I urged Grace into a canter and headed for the castle wall. As she took off, I loosened the reins to let her know we were cleared for takeoff. She seesawed perfectly over it. I focused on the next jump, and the next, and the next. Grace was sailing through the course.

Then we were at number ten—Old Hateful. Craig had suggested that the best way to boost a horse's energy was to boost my own by remembering something that challenged me. So I concentrated on outrunning that hailstorm on the prairie.

We headed for the jump and I leaned in with purpose. In the blink of an eye, we had soared over it.

We left the course clean and clear and with a pretty fast time. The five riders with the best time and no faults moved on to the jump-off. From there, whoever had the fastest time without knocking down a rail would win.

If you've ever waited to hear if your name would be announced, you know how seconds seem like hours. The announcer must have had weights on his tongue. I heard some guy's name, Valerie's name, another guy's name, Blaine's name. Then mine!

44
The Jump-off

Melanie, the only other Filly Phosphorescent entered, hadn't made the jump-off, but at least one of us was still in it. I rode over to where Whitney and the girls were sitting with big smiles on their faces. But not as big as mine.

"If I win this thing, I'll be so happy I'll…"

"Pick up a book?" Whitney suggested.

"Yes…I might even read it!"

My most likely challengers in the jump-off would be Val and the guy riding a powerful black stallion. They weren't going down without a fight. Then Craig strode over. If I had to crush on a guy who was out of my league, I'm glad he's the one I picked.

"We can't do worse than fifth place," I said.

"Don't sell yourself short, Kit. You can win this if you want."

If I want? Had he not this very morning had a run-in with the toxic troll of Silver Saddles? To finish ahead of Valerie would thrill me from the top of my manageable hair to the bottom of my double-ridged feet.

"Grace needs three things from you: speed, direction, and destination," Craig said. "Rein her in if she picks up speed between jump four and five. On the last jump, shift weight so she can use her hindquarters. The back legs are her engine."

They'd shortened the course to seven jumps for the jump-off, but four and five were still there. So was Old Hateful. Now that we had tired a little, it was looking higher and wider.

A guy named Jordan went first. He jumped the wrong gate after clearing number three, which took him out of the competition.

Then they called my number and I clicked Grace into gear. She sailed over the first three jumps like she was out for a Sunday stroll. I zeroed in on number four. Craig was right. As soon as we were over the jump, Grace began to pick up speed. I held her up just a touch then—*zoom!*—we hurdled the stone wall like a magic carpet ride.

Grace clipped her back heel on the next jump, but nothing fell. No harm, no foul! There was nothing between us and a shot at a win now except Old Hateful. I was so tuned in you could have picked me up on satellite radio.

Approach: Think hailstorm!
Takeoff: Up, up.
In the air. Weight on my heels. Forward power.
Boom! Touchdown! Rebalance. Done!

A cheering crowd sounded distant in my head. All I knew was we'd finished clean. We had to see if anyone could beat our time.

Stallion guy was next. That horse had hindquarters you could build a house on. As he started toward the last jump, I was looking to see his time when—*bang!*—the top rail on Old Hateful came crashing down. Stallion guy was out of the competition.

Blaine was next. Slow and careful will *not* win this race. She finished clean but her time was in the toilet. I almost felt sorry for her. She was going to catch holy hell from Val for being too careful.

That left only Val and her horse, Sheba. I'd never seen Val look more confident or more driven. Then she glared at me, and I'd never seen her look more like Gollum.

She and Sheba were flying around the course in total control until they got to the hedge. They had aced it the first time around. But this time, Sheba stopped short, then reared up. All of a sudden, we were at a rodeo!

Sheba started bucking inside out and upside down. I'd never seen a horse change direction in midair like that. She jumped, kicked, twisted, and whirled. To her credit, Val hung on—until she didn't.

Suddenly, she flew straight up, her arms flailing like she was swimming in air. When she finally came down, she got up and stomped away. When Blaine ran up to console her, I heard Blaine screech, "Your nose!"

After the commotion died down over Val's broken nose, the prizes were awarded. My bounty was a silver cup that I held up for the crowd to see.

Then I was stunned out of my boots. They announced that winners in each division would be attending the semifinals to be held in South Dakota!

I found Whitney's face in the crowd. Her mouth was in the shape of a frozen O. I was slated to return to South Dakota—but this time, I wouldn't be going by tree.

My big win wasn't the talk of the town, but it *was* the talk of the table at Spiro's Eatery, where we had dinner. The other Phosphorescents had left since they had three horses in trailers to get home. But Dad, Angie, and Mr. Sheppard still threw me a party, and Dad said I could invite a few friends. Since I only had a few, I invited them all.

Holly was laughing. "I can't believe I got to see a horse bounce that diva on her behind."

"Sheba's a sweet horse," I said. "She wouldn't do that for no reason."

"Maybe she got tired of being pushed around by two boots full of stupid," Whitney said.

I raised my glass to Sheba bucking off her pitiless overlord. "Today, we are all Shebas!"

We tapped our sparkling waters together. "To Sheba!"

Mr. Sheppard congratulated me, then turned to Whitney. "Don't *you* get any ideas about horse jumping. We don't have that kind of money."

Whitney scoffed. "If I ever ask you to buy me a horse, feel free to hit me in the head with a bag of oats."

"Where's your trophy?" Dad suddenly asked.

"They kept it so they can engrave my name on it…I hope they spell Higglby right."

As that sank in, Dad's mouth grew into a smile. "Does that mean you'll be keeping the name a little while longer?"

"It does," I reported. "And don't try to stop me."

"Are you still planning a European vacation next summer?" he prodded.

I scrunched up my nose as I thought of all the places the family tree could take me and said, "Maybe I can find some places around the farm to visit first."

Angie smiled. "We know one place you'll be going in a few weeks—South Dakota. Have you ever been there?"

Whitney and I sat like mannequins. Then I recovered.

"Not recently," I said, thinking of 1876.

It was getting late by the time we started home, but Main Street was alive. During tourist season, there was always something to do. Bands were playing, and pubs were crowded. Then I spotted Jonathan Rimroth and Bulldozer across from the theater, hanging out at Izzy Burgers. Those guys sure loved either burgers or movies. But this night, I didn't give a flying fig about those two turnip heads. I had a blue ribbon and a silver cup!

I thought I'd be asleep before my head hit the pillow. But my brain had other plans. As I lay in bed, my mind raced back to my Lakota grandmother. If Sesapa hadn't died so young, her children might have lived out their days on tribal lands.

How many of these other worlds are embodied in my genes? How much of the human family exists inside of me? I began to wonder what future adventures awaited me if I revisited the Higglby family tree.

I finally fell asleep, but the night didn't last long. Early the next morning, my phone rang. It was Whitney, and she was excited.

"Are you awake?"

"I am now."

"Guess who got picked to paint a mural on the Diversity Center in Stamford."

I sat up. "You're kidding! That's big time! Can I come and watch?"

"If you were here, but I'll be doing most of the painting while you're in South Dakota."

I let my head drop back on the pillow. "I've been thinking about that. I'm really not interested in show jumping. All I wanted was to beat Valerie."

"Don't forget the finals are being held at Windsor Castle in England. If you don't go, you know Valerie will finagle that trip. Why not let the last thing Wilderidge remembers about her this summer be Sheba butt-kicking her all over the stadium?"

I giggled. "I guess we owe Sheba *that* much. We may have to change their names from the Phony Ponies to the Saddle Soreheads. But wow! You get to art-paint a building in Stamford! We'll celebrate this afternoon."

It had turned out to be a pretty good summer after all.

45
The Knockdown

At breakfast, I told Dad and Angie about Whitney's mural. Angie almost did a spit take into my cornflakes.

"That is so fantastic! A local artist being honored in Stamford." Her spoon clattered to the table as she clapped her hands. "Maybe I can do a video documentary!" she shouted. "I got an award for one I made in college."

Dad barely blinked. He was used to her bursts of exhilaration. "You can unless you're going with us to South Dakota," he answered.

Her face fell. I held my hands out like I was weighing two items. "Supporting a budding young artist...or watching me jump over some fences." I let the "young artist" hand drop heavily to the table.

Angie turned to Dad. "Did anyone ever tell you you've got a great kid?"

"No one ever had to." he grinned.

I met Whitney at Popadoodle's Pizza to celebrate.

"So you got a fancy dinner, and I get a piece of Popadoodle pizza?" Whitney fake scolded.

"You haven't done any work yet. After you're famous, maybe I'll spring for two pieces. Now, what are you going to draw? I know! You could paint a mural of horses!"

"I don't think so."

"Why not? Didn't Mark Twain once say, 'There's no finer thing to paint than a horse'?"

"Not that I know of."

"Okay, I made that up. My point is, I love pictures of horses. And I think everyone else should too."

"I'm pretty sure that isn't what the Diversity Center has in mind."

"Oh yeah, I forgot that part."

Whitney tilted her head like she does when she's thinking. "But what you just said does interest me…"

After lunch, we biked over to check on the bakery expansion. Dad was on the roof of the add-on hammering nails.

"Won't be long now," he yelled down. "You know any good carpenters?"

I decided not to volunteer Fief, so we started back to Whitney's house. We only got as far as Tenth Street when we noticed two police officers on the sidewalk talking to Branca. We rode over to see what was going on as the officers left.

Branca blurted out, "Some creep knocked me off my bike and stole it."

She had bruises and scrapes on her arms and legs.

"What did the cops say?" Whitney wanted to know.

"That I'd probably never see it again. I'm not even sure they believed me," Branca said, a hint of anger in her voice.

"They know there's been a bunch of bike thefts. Why wouldn't they believe you?" I asked.

Whitney and Branca both stared at me. I finally got their drift. "Are you telling me--"

"It's what we call *Black* privilege." Whitney said and turned to Branca. "Did you see anything?"

"Not much. I think two guys were on the same bike. Then one jumped off, pushed me down, and grabbed my bike. I didn't see his face."

Branca sat down on the curb. "I guess I'm lucky I'm not dead. When he was knocking me off my bike, I thought I heard a gun go off."

"A gun?" Whitney echoed.

"Yeah, but not that loud—maybe a pop gun."

I froze. "Or like someone popping bubble gum in your ear?"

Now Branca froze. "Yeah, like that!"

"What about the other guy?" I asked.

"By the time I looked up, he'd already turned the corner—but I think his tires had blue writing on them." Branca shook her head in disgust. "What kind of jerk would knock a girl off her bicycle?"

"The kind that would help shove one into a dumpster," I said.

Whitney laser-eyed me. "You sure?"

I shook my head. "It sounds like something Rimroth and Dozer would do to be mean. But why steal the bikes? They're rich kids...although I did hear Rimroth's dad has him on a budget since the FBI's been keeping tabs on his daddy's bank accounts."

"That might explain it," Whitney nodded. "And his sidekick would do it just for sport. But we can't prove it was them."

Branca slumped. "If a councilman's kid is involved, it won't matter if we can prove it. His dad would just pull some strings and probably send *me* to jail."

I called my dad to ask if Branca could ride the bike he'd refurbished for me when I was bikeless. When he heard what happened, he promised to drop it off that afternoon.

I went home so Whitney could work on her mural design. But *my* mind was on Jonathan Rimroth. Branca was right. He'd probably get off, even if they caught him red-handed.

As I passed Izzy Burgers, guess who was riding in. The gum popper himself, Bulldozer. And right behind him, wearing a surly smile, was Jonathan Rimroth riding his bike with blue writing on the tires. They were so smug they weren't even careful.

And that's when I hatched my plan. At the dirt road, I made a right and headed for the Higglby tree.

Fief was outside the knothole, staring at a jug on the ground.

"What's going on?" I asked.

"Somebody's leaving mead out here again."

Something told me good ol' Dad had decided to carry on Great-granddad's tradition of toasting our tree.

"And guess what else?" Fief announced. "I found Taterhead. I looked his name up in the registry, and there he was!"

I was thrilled. "Is he all right?"

"Well, he's dead." Fief shrugged. "But he lived another ten years after we saw him last. He and Sassy went back to that place where we'd made camp with the Lakota and found a quiet little spot. Then, the same day Sassy died, he died too."

I entered the tree and heard Taterhead's belly laugh thundering out of Peerless's office. They were sharing some mead out of a buffalo bag. Taterhead was the happiest I'd ever seen him. But when he saw me, his smile got even bigger.

I told you I wasn't a hugger, but sometimes I can't help myself. I hugged the old man, then listened eagerly to his story.

After he died, he'd spent his time rambling around the tree swapping goods and lies with the other Higglbys.

"There's a lot of us here!" he bellowed. Then he got quiet.

"After you kids left, it warn't the same. First time in my life, I started getting lonely. Took me a partner for a while—good man. But it warn't the same. You kids were gone, then the buffalo were gone. They hauled all the Indians into them reservations, now the whole dang plains is gone." He shook his head.

"But guess what? I found out there's one of these trees for horses! Only I hear it ain't tree-shaped. It's open space with room to roam and like-a that. Someday I'm gonna go find ol' Sassy. But I've got me some family to visit first. You know, family is like a good tune—and the ones in this tree play a mighty fine melody."

I promised Taterhead we'd talk more, but right now I had a trap to spring, and I'd need help from inside *and* outside the tree.

46

The Takedown

The next morning, I waited down the street for Jonathan Rimroth to show up at Izzy's. I now knew it wasn't the movies or the burgers he liked—it was stealing bicycles. He and Dozer would scope out the best ones while the bikes' owners were catching a movie. Then they'd cut the locks, like they did on my school locker, or follow a kid home and snatch the bike that way.

I didn't have long to wait before Rimroth cruised in and checked the time. He was probably waiting for Dozer to show, so I knew I'd better move fast.

There wasn't much traffic that time of day. The only other person at Izzy Burgers was sitting at a sidewalk table, sipping a cup of coffee.

Having polished up my bike to the point of blinding brilliance, I zipped around the corner and made a flashy turn nto Izzy's. Sure enough, it got Jonathan's attention. He couldn't hold his bike envy in any longer.

"Where'd you get that bike?"

I barely gave him a glance. "It's custom-made. You couldn't afford it—you probably couldn't even ride it."

I hopped off the bike not bothering to lock it and strolled into Izzy's. The guy sipping coffee at the sidewalk table called Rimroth over. I knew what he was saying because that guy was Fief.

He was telling Jonathan he had an eye on that bike himself. And if Rimroth rode the bike to the forest where the skull-and-crossbones sign was, about twenty yards into the woods was a deer trail where someone would be waiting with a thousand dollars.

Rimroth took the bait. First, he touched the handlebars to see if he'd get shocked. When he didn't, he grabbed my bike and blasted out of Izzy's faster than a debutante out of gym class. Right on cue, Whitney rode up.

I yelled, "Hey! That guy stole my bike!" I jumped on Jonathan's bike but let Whitney do the chasing. When Jonathan saw his pursuer gaining on him, he tried to turn onto a cross street. That was where Holly was waiting.

"Hey, that isn't your bike!" she yelled.

Jonathan swerved back to Main Street. There was only one other way to turn—but sitting there on my dad's old bike was Branca, making sure Jonathan stayed on course.

Branca shouted, "Get him!" and joined the chase.

Now Jonathan had no choice but to flat-out beat them to the Forbidden Forest. He made it to the edge of town, then jumped a dry streambed in an impressive leap. He came to a stop in front of the prominent skull-and-crossbones sign.

Whitney and the gang stopped at the streambed, so Jonathan was feeling safe.

"I wouldn't come any farther! There are ghosts in here!" he yelled.

"I'm not afraid of ghosts," Whitney shouted.

"But you're about to be!" I said under my breath as I veered onto a shortcut and sped toward the deer trail.

Rimroth headed for the deer trail. He followed it for a distance, then got off my bike.

He was looking for the guy with a wad of money. But when he turned around, the only thing waiting for him was a large Viking towering over him with sword and shield.

Jonathan did what any self-respecting kid would do—he fainted like a goat. And, having arrived a few moments ahead of him, I saw it all!

Rimroth finally woke up to the hearty guffaw of one Taterhead Higglby who wanted in on the fun. But I made sure the first face Jonathan saw was mine.

"So this is what a bike thief looks like? Blink once for yes," I said.

Jonathan swallowed hard when he saw Peerless the Plunderer, Viking-at-large, looming behind me. But it was Taterhead who bent over and took all the money Jonathan had in his pocket and handed it to me.

"I hear he stole a little girl's transportation. If there's money left after she replaces it, leave it on his doorstep in a flaming bag of pig swill—I can sell you some cheap."

I turned to Rimroth. "This is Higglby property. Only our security force is allowed here."

Peerless leaned over him. "Which means you ain't! And neither is this!"

He picked up Jonathan's bike and bent it into the shape of a taco shell. That done, he picked Jonathan up and handed him the bike.

"If I ever see you or this wheelie-thing around here again, methinks you'll be wearin' it like a horse collar. Now hightail yourself out of here!"

Rimroth was gone in a flash—if said flash was dragging a tacoed bike behind it.

Later that day, I met Branca and the gang to help her pick out a new bike and to thank them for helping me kill one of my snakes—or at least make him think twice before striking again.

47

Shock and Awe

I worried about Grace being on a plane for the first time until Craig offered to travel with her and help out in Rapid City, where the event was being held.

I won't keep you in suspense. We tied for sixth place. They gave me a green ribbon—the perfect color to present to the Filly Phosphorescents.

The one thing Dad and Craig wanted to see while we were in South Dakota was Mount Rushmore. I'd seen all the mountains I wanted to see for a while, but when I realized Mount Rushmore was in the Black Hills, I got a lot more interested.

When we arrived, the place looked like a baseball game was about to start. There was a parking lot full of cars, ticket counters, cafés, and souvenir shops. Dad wanted to take the tour, which gave me a chance to ask the guide the one thing I wanted to know.

"Excuse me, do you know where a mountain called the Six Grandfathers is?"

"Right here," the guide smiled. "The Native Americans called The Six Grandfathers. But in 1885, it was renamed Mount Rushmore."

I didn't hear much else the guide said during the tour. I was busy reliving the night we spent near here, and how I saw the mirror image of the Black Hills in the constellations above. And how the Lakota followed the buffalo by tracing the celestial path through the year. And how we'd left the sacred bundle to honor Sesapa's tribe. I wondered if the bundle was still there.

I stared at the four presidential figures and understood the immense work and skill that went into sculpting them. But I was disheartened that this was the mountain Sesapa had risked her life to return to because of its spiritual connection to her people and to nature.

While Craig and Dad checked out the other exhibits, I borrowed the binoculars and walked as far as I could around the side of the mountain. I scoured the distant mountains, then put my thumb up. There it was—the two-hearts mountain! From that angle, I searched with binoculars until I saw what I thought was the crevice.

I couldn't know for sure. I will never know for sure. But just above that crevice, a bush was growing, and on it was a pink flower with quill-like thorns around it. To this day, I believe it was another message from Sesapa.

When our plane headed home, I looked out the window. I saw the enormous herds of buffalo running free, but only in my mind. I saw the Lakota people living free, but only in *their* minds. I pictured all the things in nature that have been coveted, logged, mined, and paved over, and wondered if any of them would be able to survive greed.

I also wondered which evil would last longer—greed or the condescending White worldview that brings hate and harm to others because of an obsession that all skin should be lily white.

I was grateful to Sesapa for letting me walk in her moccasins—if only for a moment in time. And I was grateful to Whitney for bringing sunlight, and starlight, into my tiny white closet that once was my entire world.

48
Favorite Colors

When I got home, I propped myself up in bed and added some KIT CONCLUSIONS:

What I once thought was a Higglby curse
turned out to be a blessing.
Higglbys may have bad hair and strange names,
but never question their heart.
◊
Sesapa believed everything in nature that is round is sacred.
I want my circle of friends to always be that to me.
◊
I've read about slavery, but I always saw it as something that
happened long ago to people far away.
It isn't, and they aren't.
◊
I'm glad my circle is getting bigger.

◊

Some traits I used to admire in old friends now seem depressing at best, disgusting at worst.

◊

Sesapa told me of a legend: When Creator placed man here with the animals, he knew man needed an animal friend to help him. But because man wasn't kind, none of the animals wanted to help.

Of all the animals, only horse said, "I will help man."

◊

Bitters 'N Sweets had a successful grand opening.
Dad and Mr. Sheppard had the bitters.
Whitney and I had the sweets.
Never eat half a cake all by yourself.

◊

Go-o-o-o-o, Higglbys!

I closed the journal and tucked myself between combed-cotton sheets in my comfy bed. But I found myself longing for the smell of a pristine forest, the sight of ponies galloping through a canyon, and chickadees hitching a ride on the back of a buffalo. Before I drifted off to sleep, the wind changed direction, and I realized that when it blows a certain way through those pine trees, the sound they make is the lonely, high-pitched whistle of Sesapa's flute.

A few weeks later, Whitney's mural was unveiled. Angie did a terrific video piece that ran on local news shows and lots of visitors came to town to see the art.

Seeing it in person was awe-inspiring. Over a surreal background, woven between her visual poetry, was lettering—gray, at first, then gradually the letters got bigger and more colorful. They read: "Color fades, but voices grow stronger."

The vibrant faces she'd painted rippled across the building canvas. All people to admire. The ones that caught my eye were Crazy Horse, Supreme Court Justice Sonia Sotomayor, and Mark Twain. And floating between those was another one I recognized…Grandmama Sheppard. And after I stared at it a little while, I'm almost sure I saw her wink.

Acknowledgments

I have a love affair with America—its geographical beauty and its ambitions.

As a history major, I developed a tremendous admiration for the most important thing our country offers—a constitution that provides peaceful ways to change bad laws and create better ones for all who live here.

Perhaps all laws would be elevated if they each started with the phrase: *In the name of human decency...*

May we continue our climb toward a more perfect union.

CPSIA information can be obtained
at www.ICGtesting.com
Printed in the USA
LVHW040244110723
752037LV00023B/466/J